PIRATE'S TREASURE

STEPHANIE FLYNN

Small Fish Publishing
Small Fish Publishing
USA

First edition
Cover design by Stephanie Flynn
ISBN ebook: 978-1-952372-41-4
ISBN paperback: 978-1-952372-39-1
ISBN hardcover: 978-1-952372-42-1
ISBN large print paperback: 978-1-952372-40-7

Also By Stephanie Flynn

Find my catalog at StephanieFlynn.com

Immortal Protector series

0.5 Vampire's Distraction

1 Vampire's Deception

2 Vampire's Secret

3 Vampire's Promise

3.5 Elf Bound

4 Vampire's Demand

Immortal Protector Side Tales

Deer Holiday

Love Claws

Depths of the Heart

Matchmaker in Time series

0.5 Minutes to Live

1 Seconds to Act
2 Hours to Arrive
3 Days to Hide
4 Years to Savor

Pirates in Time series
1 Pirate's Prize
2 Pirate's Treasure
3 Pirate's Plunder

Time Travel Romance Shorts
Fateful Time
One Crazy Time

If you like your urban fantasy without the romance, too, check out Stephanie Flynn's other name, Marie Flynn!

Special Note

While the events of this novel are fiction, the quick-witted maneuver to escape the Spanish warship awaiting the tide to capture the crew was real, performed by Calico Jack Rackham during the Golden Age of Piracy.

1

Chapter 1

ANGELA FOXE LOVED HER job until the summer crawled back to Green Bay, Wisconsin. She swiped the sweat from her forehead and palmed the steering wheel of her electric forklift, buzzing through the warehouse. When loss prevention or human resources wandered through, Angela wondered just how green the grass was on the air-conditioned side of her company.

Heading through receiving, Angela spotted Marcos between the racks, waiting to cross. She pressed the brake pedal, and with a friendly smile, she waved to him as he walked by. Their shift was almost over, and Angela was on her way to dock and recharge.

When she was a teenager, her mother needed money to help with the rent, so Angela had picked up the first job she found. Turned out, she loved to drive; it was her lifeblood. She had no need for college. She never wanted to do anything else. All things gas powered, electric powered, and if she happened upon something wind powered, she'd itch for the chance to feel its power beneath her hands. For a short while, she'd considered long-haul trucking for the bigger paycheck, but her mother's mental health declined rapidly. During a period of lucidity, her mother had told her she'd been proud of her all these years, and that still meant the world to Angela. She wouldn't give this up for air conditioning, even if it came with free donuts on Fridays. Even if it came with her fiancé being proud of her.

Brandon Spindleton was from a different world. She adored him, but after plenty of reassurance about their mismatched upbringings, she'd noticed the quips about her job. Angela expected it would take him time to unwind the thoughts he'd been engrained with since childhood. At forty years old, Angela had seen almost everything, and fully assure of who she was, Angela didn't take crap from others anymore. But those years also instilled her with plenty of empathy.

And patience for the right person who deserved it.

At the charging station, Angela turned the forklift key to the off position and climbed out. She collected her things from her locker and headed for the punch clock.

"Hey Foxe, gonna get ready for your wedding before the ceremony, or after?" Marcos called over with his stuff in his hands. Marcos was a great work friend and almost as excited about her wedding. Angela could swear he was a little bummed he didn't get to help pick out her dress.

Angela fell in stride with him, tugging at the front of her polo to fan herself. "It's tomorrow. The Spindletons have it all handled. I don't need days to wash away my warehouse sweat."

Her future mother-in-law planned the whole thing—from the location to musicians, to flowers, the color motif, and everything in between. Even her dress. Angela only needed to show up clean for the hairstylist, makeup artist, and tailor to work their magic. She'd always pictured an intimate beach wedding, not an opulent affair at a grand estate, but this was one of many compromises Angela had made. Brandon took a while to ease off on his comments about their differences; Angela allowed the elder woman much more grace.

Sometimes sacrifices had to be made for the greater good. In this case, keeping mother-in-law happy. All Angela cared about was beginning her life with her future husband.

At the far wall by the exterior door, Marcos swiped his badge through the card reader, and the little machine beeped to end his shift. "Every bride I ever met needed several days to dress and several more to shout at people, but not you. Oh, no! Foxe can walk down the aisle covered in dust and still look radiant."

"Suck up." Angela's cheeks heated. She appreciated Marcos, one of the few people in her life who didn't raise brows at her and Brandon's mismatched relationship. Or outright assume she was a gold digger. Angela hated that.

Marcos cracked up laughing.

"But *gracias*," Angela added.

"I'm surprised Mrs. Spindleton didn't lock you in a room of her estate to make sure you didn't run away."

The Spindleton estate rested on the top of a grassy knoll overlooking the whole small town not far from the city limits. Angela didn't have to be locked inside to assure she'd show. The home was stunning, and she loved Brandon. They'd been together long enough to know each other's faults and love each other despite them. And even with different upbringings, they agreed on many hot-button issues, which truthfully surprised her. Brandon was not what most people assumed. He was a good guy, loyal, handsome as hell, and most importantly, he loved her. And when she was with him, she felt like a princess.

"His mother trusts me. I'll see you tomorrow."

"You won't recognize me in a suit. That man better spoil you good," Marcos said.

Angela swiped her badge, too. She *was* spoiled a little. Brandon bought her small gifts; nothing too fancy, but certainly more than she needed. Mrs. Spindleton was tight with the trust fund, but Angela didn't care about his money. "I'm so spoiled, I'm rotten. I can't wait to see you."

Marcos pushed through the door to the parking lot of the warehouse, and Angela followed since they'd parked next to each other. They squinted into the sunlight, and Marcos beamed, his teeth shining bright white against his dirty skin. "Find me. I might not recognize you without all your dirt."

"Just look for the dress." Her future mother-in-law chose the dress to match the Spindleton legacy of elegance, grace, and luxury. Knowing the woman, Angela figured the elder chose a similar style gown for herself. "On second thought, I'll be in a white dress and a veil. Make sure you find the veil first."

"Will do." Marcos's friendly smile slid away.

Something was wrong. Angela had to ask. "Did you forget to have your socks pressed?"

"I heard things about Brandon." Marcos waved the air dismissively. "It's nothing. Everyone hears things about him. If there was any truth to the rumors, you'd have discovered them."

Oh, she'd heard that concern before. Emily Porter, her best friend, mentioned those same rumors. Her mother mentioned it too, but Angela explained how click-bait articles worked. But still, after enough people worrying, what were they seeing that she wasn't? Angela stopped at her car door. Marcos was right. If there was something suspicious about Brandon, she would've figured it out by now.

"You have nothing to worry about."

The smile returned. "I thought so. *Adiós.*" Marcos waved as he opened his driver's side door.

Angela waved back and dropped into her own driver's seat. Good thing marriages were about the spouse and not the family. She cleaned her fingers with the front of her polo before pulling out her cell phone. She sent a text to Brandon, asking to spend time with him tonight.

His bachelor party was a few nights ago, so he didn't have an excuse tonight. Angela's had been last week, hosted by Mrs. Spindleton. Angela, her tween future sister-in-law, and teenage future cousin-in-law, shared tea and watched a movie. Admittedly, it was dull. At least Emily Porter and Robin Hall had taken her out for drinks at the local dive bar. It wasn't as fun as their camping trips, but any time with Emily and Robin was a good time.

Angela asked her other friends if they wanted to throw her a bachelorette, but they'd declined. Emily explained the women snubbed their noses at Angela for not inviting them to be her bridesmaids. Angela didn't get to pick her bridesmaids. Brandon dismissed her concerns, explaining everyone acted out of character during the stress of weddings. His reason made sense to her, but the cold-shoulder stung, nonetheless.

A reply came back from Brandon on her screen. '*Not tonight. Too busy getting ready for tomorrow. Get your beauty rest.*'

They'd been together for over a year, and she still hadn't met his friends outside of one appearance at a fine dining event at the estate. So Angela knew they existed, but she didn't know any of them. Angela pressed, '*After all this time, can't I join you for one night of drinks?*'

'*Guy time, sorry.*'

Angela gritted her teeth. She worked with men doing arguably a man's job. What about her wasn't appropriate for his friends? Even the local news wouldn't care if she went out with the guys for a night. And even if some rookie reporter didn't know better, they were the Spindletons! They were capable of stopping whatever bad press they wanted. It didn't make any sense. Every relationship had its flaws, and hers was no exception. If not for this one silly but frustrating flaw, Brandon Spindleton was a great guy, and she was lucky to have him.

2

Chapter 2

West Indies, 1715

Captain Henry Price. Captain, he kept repeating to himself. The word was still foreign on his tongue. This crew of bilge rats actually chose him to lead. He supposed they'd appreciated his efforts as the quartermaster—being a stickler for the rules and keeping the captain's whims in line. But quartermaster was a different role from captain, opposing in fact. Now Price was the leader of the whims. Although he'd daydreamed of the possibilities of this position, they were simply that—musings of an angry man.

Musing as such, no sane man would've voted for.

A knocking on his cabin door pulled him from his planning. Price dragged a hand through his hair and replaced the cocked hat on his head. "Come in."

Price never trusted a skinny cook. How could the palate of a thin man know what was tasty and what wasn't? The experience was in his size, and Giles had decades of it. "Captain, as much as I love our quartermaster, I wanted to take this issue to you directly."

Price clasped his hands together as the ship beneath them glided across the sparkling sea. To Price's forty years, the new quartermaster, Noah Riley, was a boy at six and twenty. He'd earned his votes for his charisma and friendliness. But Price was concerned his age wouldn't suit, and now Giles's worries had him extra troubled. "What is it?"

"May I speak plainly?"

Captain Price gestured for him to continue.

"Sir, Captain Lemoine struggled to reign in his crew, because working men will never be amiable with hardtack and a dribble of rum."

"I agree, but that's no longer an issue. We can afford provisions."

Captain Eric Lemoine had secured riches from the sunken Spanish treasure galleon off the coast of Florida, and most of the crew retired. Even crusty Hyde and the frustrating Hooper. Price had more than a man's share himself, but when the current account wasn't sufficient, he gladly offered the gold out of his own funds to fill it. The money wasn't why he hunted these waters.

"We can, but the last prize was mostly tobacco. Unless we return to Nassau to sell it, or pay a visit to a nearby settlement soon, we shall find an agitated crew once again."

That wouldn't do. Price couldn't lose time returning home, but he couldn't continue with an unsettled crew. Not with the plans he had. "Show me."

It was sunny with strong winds, and yet the ocean toyed with them, reminding them of its fickle whims, not too unlike the crew itself. These men were made for the sea, understood it, communed with it, respected it. Price simply used it.

Captain Price followed his cook below deck of the *Sea Lion*, into the murky and oft-unpleasant smelling lower levels. Sunlight filtered down through the companionways and open portholes, but he and Giles carried candles. The hold was much darker—a secure room meant for keeping their most prized possessions, including food and water.

At the door to the hold, Giles braced himself against a swell, tossing the ship to starboard. Price leaned with the force and kept himself upright. Water splashed down from above, and Price cradled the candle flame so it wouldn't drown out. When he finished the task he'd been planning for months, he never wanted to see the ocean or feel the hollow swish of his stomach again.

He belonged on land, where his old friend currently retired to. Lemoine hadn't left because he'd been satisfied with his gold. No, he left because he'd found a woman—a strange woman, willing to deceive the crew to her own ends. She'd broken the rules, and Price had to punish her for it. Secretly, he admired her gumption and was relieved Lemoine offered to take her lashes. Price hadn't known she was a woman at the time, but looking back on it, he would've been sick flogging her. What kind of woman had the strength to take on a pirate crew and live to tell about it? Price smiled to himself. He'd never found someone who challenged him and interested him at the same time. Maybe there was someone out there for him.

If his brother could hear the thoughts in his head right now, he'd be laughed at and slapped for losing his senses. William Price was a wise man. Just as his musings over taking the captaincy had filled his daydreams then, a nonexistent woman filled his daydreams now. Such a waste of time! A certain Spaniard captain had to answer for his crimes, because murder could not go unanswered.

The ship groaned and tilted, as if agreeing, and the men braced themselves. "A mighty storm approaches from the east. Any port for restocking is preferable."

"I'll take your advisement under consideration," Price said, dryly.

As the ship returned to level, Giles wiped sweat from his brow. "See there, captain?" The cook pointed to the barrels in the corner of the hold, but their candlelight didn't penetrate far enough.

"What am I seeing, exactly?" Barrels and crates were neatly stacked. Nothing stood out to him as unacceptable.

Giles squeezed through and lifted a lid of a barrel to prove his concerns. Tobacco. Another lid—more tobacco from their latest prize. Price asked, "Is it all tobacco?"

"The French crew knew they were losing, so they dumped the food just to spite us. Money's great, but you can't eat it. Or at least, I haven't figured how to cook it. We should return home, sell our prize, restock, and we'll avoid this storm." Giles gave a wry smile.

Price had taught their captain a lesson that day, but lessons didn't fill empty stomachs either. Not a satisfied man could live off crumbs alone. The cook was right in his worry. "We shall restock in Cuba."

"Cuba? Captain, Nassau is closer, and I daresay, safer?"

True, an island roaming with lawless thieves was safer than a settled society. Hunters like them called Nassau home, a city on the free island of New Providence. Cuba was Spanish territory, a fearsome, well-funded enemy, especially to Captain Price.

"How many weeks of food do we have aboard?"

"Weeks? Oh, captain, two at most, and I have a few days' worth of potatoes, and then we're back on hardtack."

That was the perfect excuse Price needed. "A few days of potatoes isn't enough to return to Nassau, and safer doesn't matter if the crew squabbles among themselves. We'll restock in Cuba and ride out the storm."

"Can we sell the tobacco in Cuba?" Giles asked.

The cook's concern was worth noting. Enemies didn't barter with each other, but Price wasn't going to drop his course. "Reduce the rations enough to stretch it to three weeks."

"Yes, captain," Giles said, defeat in his tone, and he left for the galley, taking his candle with him, casting shadows along his unsteady path.

While Price was down here in the hold, and had the free moment, he wanted to prevent more issues like this before they landed at Cuba. Riley's job was to keep inventory, but the man was busy at the moment, and old habits were hard to correct. If Price had done the inventory himself after their last prize, he wouldn't be caught in this conundrum. Price pulled a pad of paper out of his fine coat pocket and closed the door to the hold behind him.

A wave rocked the *Sea Lion*, a formidable ship in the best weather and trustworthy in the worst. An angry storm, approaching to test the ship's strength, stood between him and his personal enemy on Cuba. Price headed straight into it, because sailing the long way around meant they'd run out of food, and turning around meant he'd lose his one chance.

3

Chapter 3

Wearing jeans and a scratchy polo most days, Angela Foxe appreciated a chance to dress up and feel cute, but this was way beyond her comfort zone. Angela sat on a hand-carved stool in front of a dainty vanity, while her future sister- and cousin-in-law doted on her makeup and hair. Mrs. Spindleton supervised behind them while putting out fires with the wedding planner through text. As thick locks fell into her face and a brush swiped at her cheeks, Angela closed her eyes against the foreign barrage of pampering.

"One long year and it's finally going to happen." Mrs. Spindleton said, wearing a sky-blue pencil skirt and matching blazer. Pearls draped around her lined neck. Frankly, Angela was surprised the lady of the house had chosen something so...appropriate. "And here we never thought Brandon would settle down. At least he found you."

Angela smiled with closed lips and pressed her arms against the cape protecting her dress—an intricately beaded blue and white gown. It reminded her of the flowers decorating the ceremony room—orchids and white lilies. They were scented, sweeter than a department store's perfume section. She focused on the scent, a safety net to guide her through this day. Soon the pomp and circumstance would be over, and then Angela could live her life with her husband.

"I'm glad we got that prenup situation settled," Mrs. Spindleton continued. "What a stressful time that was!"

When Angela was twelve years old, her mother cheated and her parents divorced. Angela had spent one week at her mother's and the next at her father's before bouncing back again. Neither house felt like home, and most of her life was stored in a duffel bag she carried back and forth. Each of her parents remarried shortly thereafter and started a new family of their own. Angela was an inconvenience, a burden to be brushed aside, until that relieving moment she turned eighteen and started her own life.

The Spindletons didn't mind her less-than-lofty background, but in order for Mrs. Spindleton to allow the engagement to commence, Angela had to sign away all rights to any of the Spindleton estate. Angela's mother, during a moment of clarity, had snubbed her nose at the publicized family, rambling on about trust and tightwads. She'd recall scandals she knew had happened, but the media buried it. Her father didn't offer an opinion either way, but she didn't get much out of him, regardless. He'd never outright said it to her face, but Angela suspected she reminded him too much of his cheating wife, and couldn't stand to see her. Angela had never been doted on by a loving father, so when the Spindletons opened their arms to her, she'd thought she'd won at life.

Truthfully, the Spindleton money made her nervous. She didn't want to be sued by her future mother-in-law for knocking over a vase in the hallway with her wedding gown. So she wasn't upset at the pre-nup, but she'd be lying if she wasn't hurt a little. Then she was handed another document to sign, something called a non-disclosure agreement, for whatever reason. Angela never fed the press anything, no matter how much they...pressed. Angela never had a loving family where she felt accepted, so when the Spindletons asked her to sign, Angela considered that a minor roadblock to finally having found love.

Powder fell onto her cheek from Charlotte's brush. The girl used a pinkie finger to dash it away. Angela practiced shallow breaths to prevent herself from sneezing.

"When is your last day at work?" Mrs. Spindleton asked. "We need to have a small celebration. Nothing like this, of course, something quieter."

Uh, that was news to her. "What do you mean?"

"Hold still," Charlotte asked politely.

The excitement drained from the lady's pale face. "Oh, dear. Brandon never mentioned it? Or the attorney? The documents you signed included a clause requiring you to resign. No Spindleton in this family works at—"

"I'm not quitting," Angela interrupted with a cocked brow. "And no one ever mentioned it." Angela had conceded nearly everything the woman demanded, but that was too far. Perhaps Brandon didn't mention it because her employer didn't bother him. A flush of warmth settled in her chest.

"Oh, I see," the elder Spindleton said gravely.

The girls exchanged looks and private smiles, while Mrs. Spindleton focused on her phone. The woman texted with a vengeance.

The family had always been strict with appearances, but Angela figured by allowing her to marry Brandon, they'd eased a little. Her assumption appeared to be wrong, and Angela worried if she'd just screwed up her only chance at happiness.

Angela's cell phone rang, but since she was busy 'holding still', she ignored the call.

At forty, the dating pool was shrinking fast, and Angela wasn't a pampered teenager, never had been. From lifting and carrying cases of merchandise and climbing in and out of the forklift, Angela was built stronger than most women her age. And she exercised and lifted weights at the gym on the regular. Her hands were calloused, and her arms were broad. If she was inclined to brag, she had calves of iron. Despite all the hard work involved in maintaining her shape, her favorite feature was her long brunette hair, which she cared for and pampered harder than the Spindleton's dog.

Except Katherine was burning it with the curling iron.

"Stop moving!" Charlotte squeaked. The girl's dream was to become a makeup artist, but her mother forbade it, since the Spindletons were above all menial service work, and apparently Angela's fit that category like a mole needing to be excised. Well, Angela happened to like her spots, and that one was staying. She'd have Brandon explain it to her.

"You need to move!" The teenage Katherine argued with her younger cousin while flipping wefts of Angela's hair around a heated barrel.

"I can't get anything done with your arms in my way," Charlotte countered. And the bickering resumed.

Angela chuckled and rubbed beads of her gown between her fingers. Such delicate fine work. So dainty, so detailed, so...expensive. Everything Angela wasn't.

"Girls, girls, enough," Mrs. Spindleton scolded, sliding the phone back into her handbag. "How is Angela supposed to be relaxed on the biggest day of her life, with you two arguing in her ear?"

"Sorry, mother," Charlotte said.

"Sorry, Mrs. Spindleton." Katherine released a curled lock.

Both girls were monotone in their apologies as if it were a common occurrence. Their instant obedience irked Angela. The girls hadn't done anything wrong. They were just kids—passionate kids whose interests should be nurtured, not smothered.

Angela's phone rang again inside the matching beaded purse resting on the vanity. With a frown, she lifted it out and found several missed calls and four texts. She sighed and swiped her screen with only minor protests from Charlotte and a stink-eye from the girl's mother. Since calling would interfere with her hair being styled, Angela opened the first text message and read. Then she scrutinized the tiny photograph included and reread, disbelief and confusion growing. She covered the screen with her hand, and she stood, despite the protests.

"I need a minute alone, okay?"

Mrs. Spindleton nodded. "Come, girls. Give the bride some air."

Katherine set down the curler and turned it off, and the girls left the room with the lady of the house.

Angela paced in her satin high heels. Organza danced, and the chiffon swished with her steps. Beads swirled and shimmered. Up until she'd woke her phone screen, she'd felt like a princess. Now Angela had a sinking feeling her precarious crown was about to shatter.

Angela stared wide-eyed at her phone.

'He *did this behind my back*,' the anonymous text read. '*Just thought you should know before it's too late.*'

Angela tapped the image to download, and filling her smartphone screen was a nude image of Brandon with a woman she'd never met. First, Angela searched the surroundings. Where was this? She didn't recognize the room, but it was clearly a bedroom and not up to the Spindleton's standards. Then Angela looked at the clothes on the floor, but she couldn't make them out. She checked Brandon's haircut and facial hair. He hadn't worn that buzzed style with a trimmed beard in a while. This image couldn't have been recent. Angela calmed down. Just an ex jealous of her wedding, but something tickled in the back of her mind, and Angela indulged in the curiosity.

'*When was this?*' Angela texted back.

'*Two years ago. We fought because he only wanted to spend time with his friends and not me.*'

That sounded familiar.

'*Then I found out why. He's a cheater who keeps proof instead of burying it. BS warned me if I questioned his actions, he'd share the image with everyone I knew, and tell them he was the victim of lies and Photoshop to destroy me. I wasn't the first. You won't be the last. You'll know he's lying when he first claims he was single at the time this was taken. He most definitely wasn't, and if you argue, then he doubles down with image editing.*'

Angela's heart thundered in her chest like stampeding horses. Her fiancé did have many relationships before her, according to the local tabloids, but this...this was so far out there, she couldn't believe it. *'If he's a cheater, why did he threaten you with blackmail?'*

'Since he went out with friends all the time with no accountability, I decided I could too, but he didn't like that. He didn't like his reputation tarnished publicly. His mother is scary.'

Angela understood that.

'He forbid me from having my own life. All BS cares about his having fun, and he knows no bounds if he believes anyone disobeys him. It's an obsession. I still get messages from him warning me to keep my mouth shut. Threatening me with defamation and legal fees.'

It was almost too wild to believe. Besides, if his mother was that scary, and he was that much of a control freak, Brandon would've said something about her menial job.

'I never heard this reported,' Angela texted. Small towns knew everything about everyone. No whispers resembling anything like this floated around the social scene.

'And you never will. We all signed NDAs. Just like you probably did. Sorry.'

NDA. Non-disclosure agreement. This was about keeping Angela a prisoner in her own life to bolster Brandon's reputation. He had the freedom to do whatever he wanted and cared nothing for the woman he supposedly loved. And he would threaten and lash out for years at those who'd made mistakes in his family's eyes.

A cheater being a cheater was doubtful, but this whole vengeance obsession was absolutely crazy, and nothing at all like the Brandon she knew. This had to be some weird jealousy thing from an ex. Angela had known the

Spindletons were capable of stopping whatever bad press they wanted.

The doubt lingered.

Angela stared at the screen, hands shaking. Right now, in a room down the wing, Brandon dressed in his tuxedo with all his groomsmen—whom she had never properly met. The final words repeated in her head. 'We *all signed* NDAs.' Angela sure did. The attorneys covered Brandon's shenanigans over the years, and they knew enough to enforce an NDA ahead of time. But the women keep tabs on him, warning each new love of his life.

Angela couldn't believe she'd been so oblivious. The mystery woman's reason for their fight rang true. Brandon never invited her along with his friends. Like she was some toy he collected from the shelf, dusted off, and entertained himself with for a short while, before returning it to its place.

With the picture on her phone as proof, Angela opened the boudoir door and called down the hall, "Mrs. Spindleton, I need a word with you."

The old woman cruised around the corner with her daughter and niece in tow. "Good timing. The guests are seated, and the musician is ready to begin shortly. We must finish getting you presentable." Her sunken eyes raked her head to her hem, and the excitement waned. "You didn't get makeup on your dress, did you?"

Angela held out a hand, stopping the girls. "I need a minute alone, okay?"

The girls looked to the head of the house, who nodded, and they turned and walked away. Angela waved Mrs. Spindleton into the room.

"What's the matter?" she asked.

Angela held out the photo on her screen, and the woman gasped, hand covering her mouth as if the photo of her son's naked rear disturbed her delicate eyes.

"Where did you get that?"

"A woman sent it to me. She claims Brandon cheated on her. Do you know anything about this?"

Mrs. Spindleton bristled. "That's a lie, I tell you! She used the computer to alter that image."

Angela double checked the photo. "You're telling me this *isn't* Brandon? Someone glued his face on this picture just to upset me?"

Mrs. Spindleton's brow furrowed. "Those useless damned attorneys! What good are they? Who was it? I'm going to bury..." With a final angry gaze, Mrs. Spindleton rolled her eyes, as if further conversing with Angela was a waste of her time. The elder Spindleton fished out her cell phone and dialed. When the ringing stopped, she said, "I need Arnold on the line immediately."

It was true. It was all true.

While Mrs. Spindleton continued ranting at the useless attorney, Angela collected her purse off the vanity and left the room. The girls had already busied themselves somewhere else, and Angela was thankful to avoid that awkward conversation.

Down the hall, swishing along on the hand-woven Persian rugs, Angela stopped at the door to the groom's chambers, exhaled a deep breath, and barged into the room.

Brandon stood in front of a tri-folding floor-length mirror, while the groomsmen in their tuxes hovered around him, leaning to see his phone screen. The men held open bottles of beer, and laughter filled the room. A gray-haired man in a dress shirt and pants with a tape measure around his neck kneeled at the hem of Brandon's pants, making last-minute adjustments.

Brandon noticed her entrance and blocked his hands from his eyes like an immature child. "Whoa, honey. It's bad luck to see the bride in her gown before the ceremony. You know that."

Angela marched right up to him, splitting the groomsmen, whose laughter died, and she held the incriminating photo to his face. "Care to explain this?"

The groomsmen whispered to each other, and Brandon dropped the levity. Her fiancé leaned over and squinted at her screen. The tailor at his feet made a noise when Brandon shifted. Angela didn't care about how even the hem was.

Brandon's face drained of color. "How did you...?" His whispered tone of disbelief had Angela question herself. Had this woman set her up? She was too angry at all of it to turn her cheek now. She needed the truth, regardless of the consequences.

"The mysterious woman in this provocative pose"—Angela tilted her head, admiring the angle—"sent me a text this morning. Is it true?" She wanted to hear it from his mouth.

"Sir, I insist," the tailor urged, tugging at the hem.

"If he doesn't explain," Angela told the tailor, "then your efforts are a waste."

At her clear warning, Brandon bristled. "You're considering throwing away our future because some bimbo ex-girlfriend texted you a pic of us?"

"The bimbo ex-girlfriend, as you call her"—What would he call Angela?—"said this woman wasn't her. You cheated and used it against her. Is that true?"

Brandon's face pinched with fury. "I wasn't with Brooke when this was taken. She lied, and you're willing to trust her word over mine? I thought we were stronger than that."

"Are you telling me you were single when this photo was taken?" Angela deliberately used the catchphrase to see if this mystery Brooke was right.

"Exactly. I'm glad you could see reason." Brandon smiled and leaned in for a kiss, but Angela leaned away. Brandon shifted his weight, covering for the failed kiss. Didn't want to be embarrassed in front of his precious friends. He cleared his throat and added, "I knew you were always a smart cookie. Now get out of here before you jinx our wedding."

A rock filled Angela's chest, pressing harder and harder with each of Brandon's lies and excuses. In a flash, one of the groomsmen grabbed Brandon's phone and tossed it to her. The tailor kneeling at Brandon's feet blocked his attempt to take it back from her.

Angela lit up the screen to see just what they'd been sharing when she walked in. With Brandon's hair, necklace, and clothes, she recognized exactly when this was taken. Brandon was elbow-deep in another woman just a few days ago. "Who is she?"

"This stuff always happens at bachelor parties. It's almost the rules," Brandon said dismissively.

The groomsman who'd whispered to others now tugged on a couple of the men's tuxes to signal them to leave. Several of the groomsmen sent her a look of pity.

Tears filled her lids, and the rock crushed harder, making breathing difficult. All these men knew what Brandon was doing. She glared at each one as they walked out in shame.

Alone, Brandon shook off the grouchy tailor and closed his hands over hers. "You know me, Angela. This whole thing... Those women... They didn't mean anything. I didn't love any of them, but I love you. I would never do anything to hurt you."

Angela gave herself a minute to steady her voice. "You already did."

"No, no, honey. It was an innocent mistake. I promise it will never happen again. We'll walk down that aisle together and start fresh, a new beginning, just you and me." Brandon squeezed her hands tighter, crushing the phones against her skin. She would've cried out in pain if she weren't already hurting too much to feel it.

Angela wished she could throw the phones in the garbage and never see them again. She wished she never seen another phone again in her life. Remembering all the good times they'd shared, she wanted to believe him, but she just couldn't.

"You were going to use that photo against me as blackmail if I ever disobeyed, weren't you? And you'd fixate on my punishment for years. Why?"

Brandon released her hands, and the sweet act slid from his face. A smirk appeared, and Angela squeezed his phone, wishing it was his neck.

"When you're someone like me, people come from all walks of life to take advantage. This is my way of not only preventing that but also enjoying the process. A personal insurance plan, if you will. You should be proud. I didn't set up this photo until just before our wedding. There really was something special about you. Everyone else got theirs much earlier."

Was. She heard it straight from his mouth, not that she'd ever consider reconciling. Too disgusted for words, Angela hurled his phone at the tri-fold mirror, cracking the screen and the glass, and hopefully destroying both. The tailor ducked and covered his head. Angela turned on her expensive heels and marched toward the door.

"Don't tell anyone about this," Brandon called after her. "You already signed the NDA. Brook's in big trouble with Arnie, and you don't want to join her."

Angela slammed the heavy door behind her and rushed down the hallway. Tears filled her eyes, and the edge of her chiffon snagged on a decorative table. With a wet sniffle, Angela yanked on it, not caring if the fabric tore, but a vase probably worth more than her car tipped over and shattered.

4

Chapter 4

Months later, Angela Foxe didn't know what to expect, but silence wasn't it. A stiff dude in a suit had arrived and collected her dress. Otherwise, attorneys had buried the scandal once again. Brooke never responded to texts about what happened, as if she fell off the face of the earth. It was eerie. Angela thought she knew the man she loved and trusted. Sure, Brandon's family was stuffy and uptight, but she couldn't blame them. They had a legacy to protect and assets to hide. Still, no more prenups and uptight mothers-in-law for her. And no more expensive vases taunting her into bankruptcy.

Angela was free, watching out for *numero uno*.

That was what she'd told herself in between bouts of ice cream and candies, wallowing in the loss of yet another family—rejected by her parents, rejected by Brandon and his family. She couldn't help but wonder what was wrong with her. Why wasn't she anyone's *numero uno*? When her confidence returned, Angela attempted to date, but no one ever went anywhere. How could she trust her date wasn't the next Brandon in disguise? Her judgment, along with her heart, was irreparably broken.

Emily had told her, 'Don't dismiss the entire sea because of one rotten fish.' The woman was right, statistically speaking, but Angela was too old to play games, so casual fun was her hard line. Hot guys only and one night only were the rules.

Marcos had been disappointed he didn't get to see her dress, but when he'd delivered a boatload of candy and a bottle of wine to her door, he bashed the Spindletons long enough to get over it. Angela even laughed a few times.

Now life was good. Life was simple. She had no complaints until Emily was destroyed by that greedy ass Tyler. Now a broke history buff, Emily needed someone to fill his ticket at the Tall Ships festival, so it would go to waste. History wasn't Angela's thing. She was quite content to leave the past where it belonged. But when Emily promised to go anywhere of Angela's choosing next, she reluctantly murmured her consideration. And when Emily had said many hot guys would be at the festival, some dressed like Captain Jack Sparrow, Angela agreed, excited to find a perfectly skimpy outfit.

Angela picked out a pirate wench costume. It was ruffly and short in the front and reached her calves in the back. The neckline was off the shoulder, with a sexy brown corset on the outside to push the assets up. She curled and pinned her long brunette hair away from her face in a romantic half updo, and covered it with a lacy, black tricorn hat with a pinch of feathers. But the boots were the best part. Black, knee-height, and cuffed. Although, walking with the pointed heels in the grass wasn't as easy as she'd expected. But Angela looked hot, and she planned to find herself a captain for the evening.

None of the early festival visitors had caught her attention, but the next best distraction—outside of alcohol—was shopping, and a particular vendor table enthralled her. In the farthest row, away from the others, a hunched old woman sold the most beautiful, handcrafted jewelry. She offered them special necklaces from a locked chest—amethyst on a copper chain—for a ridiculously low sum of five bucks. Angela couldn't turn them down.

None of that was weird.

In fact, Angela was having a great time as Emily led her up the gangway and onto the first tour ship. Lines were strung all over the ship and wrapped around massive cleats. The sails were furled to prevent the ships from moving in the breeze. This might've been Emily's scene, but a silly smile lifted Angela's lips. Angela scanned the deck for the ship's wheel. Maybe the tour company would let her sail it for a little while. Or at least pretend?

"Ladies, packages are not allowed." A tour guide, wearing a clean-pressed plain uniform, approached from behind them. "There's a basket on land to store belongings." With his hands clasped behind his back and his chest puffed, the employee continued his patrol on deck.

That was a little weird.

Angela and Emily glanced over the rail. Just off the ship was a large crate guarded by a man with a bored look on his face.

"I'm not leaving this behind to get stolen!" Angela whispered. The necklace was cheap, but uniquely beautiful.

"Me neither. He didn't say we couldn't wear them." Emily shrugged.

"True." Angela and Emily dug their necklaces out of their shopping bags and slipped them over their heads.

But this, this was very weird. What the hell?

ANGELA HAD BOARDED A replica antique pirate ship for a cruise...for tourists, filled with men and women in clean, machine-stitched uniforms and modern hairstyles. In the blink of an eye, the ship workers had disappeared, and Angela found herself below deck in a suffocating room with only a porthole for light and a stench reminding her of the meat department's expired waste. A strong scent of tobacco hit her nose and then the faintest odor of charred wood. The ship rocked and groaned. How did she get down here? And why was it rocking? It had been secured to the dock with calm waters.

Angela hadn't partaken in alcohol lately. Was she experiencing blackouts while sober? Blackouts...jumps in time...missing memories. Angela's stomach sank. Those were the first signs of her mother's illness. Angela was forty years old. She'd expected to inherit the detrimental gift, but not for many years yet. How could it be happening already with such a severe leap?

Voices. Men were in here talking. Angela ducked behind barrels, holding her breath like a trespasser about to get busted. Gulls outside cawed like an alarm. She didn't want to get in trouble for being in a restricted area and ruining Emily's good time. She pressed herself lower, trying to keep her hands off the floor. The balls of her feet ached.

The men talked about Cuba, or something. Must be their next stop when they finished with the Great Lakes. Angela could hardly hear over the noise of the birds, the waves sloshing the ship, and the pounding of the barrel lids and her heart.

A heavy man's footsteps faded. He left. Angela listened to see if she was alone, and she didn't hear anything. She poked her head up above the barrel. A man held a candle in his hands, flickering yellow light over his handsome features. Angela smiled at the defined and stubble-covered jaw, angled Cupid's bow, and strong brow. It glinted over the gold stud in his ear. Where else did he have jewelry? He was exactly what she'd been looking for, but the man's clothing was unusual. Emily had warned her ship workers and visitors alike could 'get into' the pirate lifestyle.

This striking man wore a dark coat with gold buttons and a white neckerchief dangling over an ivory vest. Angela couldn't be certain in the lighting, but she thought breeches covered his thighs. He appeared to be her age. In his hand was a pad of paper, and he scrawled on a sheet as he maneuvered around the room. He was taking inventory! A hot flash rocked her body. Was it from the inventory process or an incredibly attractive, distinguished man?

Angela took off her frilly hat and forced herself to stay hidden. The leather pack clipped around her waist, containing her credit cards, stayed secured. Watching him, Angela's heart pounded in her ears. Why was she hiding? She wasn't a shy woman, and this guy was going to be her next fun fling—if he was willing, of course. Before standing and introducing herself, another man hollered from the other side of the door. Her sexy pirate turned his head. His dark brown hair was layered and shoulder length, something she didn't often anymore, and it was sexy as hell.

"What's the matter, Karl?" His voice was lilted with an English accent, and Angela swooned so hard she thought her corset buttons were going to pop off.

The man stepped closer and closer, scratching on the paper, until he stopped on the other side of the barrel from her. Angela ducked lower, holding her breath to stay silent, but her pounding heart and swishing blood in her ears were going to get her caught.

The voice was muffled, and with a grunt of annoyance from her sexy pirate, he left, taking the candle with him. Darkness returned and Angela's eyes adjusted to a single flashlight's worth of daylight filtering in through a smudged porthole. She still hadn't seen Emily. With the crew out of sight, Angela whispered, "Em? Are you here?"

No answer. Of course not. If Emily was in here, she would've dived at the pirate and asked him history questions. Just as Angela would've dived at him and asked questions about sailing this ship, but she didn't. Angela lifted up on her knees, craning her head around to see where Emily hid.

"This isn't funny. Come out."

Still, Emily wouldn't answer. This wasn't funny at all. Only the groans of the ship and rocking from the lake's waves returned her plea. Angela rubbed her elbow on the porthole glass to clean it and peered out. Her face scrunched. Those were big waves for Lake Michigan. The color of the water was off, and no land was in sight. How was that possible? From any location on the lake, some land formations could be seen. She hadn't been on the ship long enough for the crew to have navigated out of Lake Michigan, and that wasn't part of the tour. More concerning were the angry clouds on the horizon. What the...?

Angela stood up with a frown. The ship bucked into a wave, and Angela grasped the hull for balance as water splashed the porthole and rained down on her from the decks above. With a grimace, she swiped away the water from her face, but it felt off—wrong.

Warm.

Sticky.

She tasted it before thinking of all the surfaces it had just passed through. Salty? The Great Lakes weren't salty.

Angela climbed her way through the stacks of barrels, trying her best to avoid knocking anything over with the swaying of the ship and poor lighting. "Em, this isn't funny anymore. Where are you? Something's not right." She searched every inch of the hold to make sure Emily wasn't knocked out by something loose. This ship was worse than an amusement park ride, and her stomach flipped with the foreign sensation.

Emily wasn't in here.

Well, Angela wasn't going to stay down here and wait for trouble to find her. She pushed through the door and, keeping her head ducked from the uncomfortably low ceiling, she found a ladder. The stink of garbage or sewage hit her nose harder over here. Her eyes watered. For a paying customer, this tour ship was disgusting. How did she let Emily talk her into this? If she found Emily above deck flirting with the captain, oh, Angela was going to need a lot of schmoozing to make it up to her.

Angela climbed up just high enough to poke her head out. Men pulled lines and climbed the rigging, while others conversed in small groups. Not a single one appeared to be an employee of the tour company. Salty sea air blew in her face, whipping her dampened locks over her shoulder. As a group closed the distance, she noted pistols at their waistbands and...swords? Dirty, nicked, and way too real. Angela's upper lip curled in disbelief.

These guys were hardcore pirate fans. When Emily emerged from wherever she hid, she was in for a treat. And then Angela was giving her a tongue lashing.

"You there! Oy! You! What are you doing 'ere?" A man from a small group pointed at her with a snarl on his dirt-streaked face—honest disgust she hadn't seen since...Brandon's hateful confession. He wore a bandanna around his head of shaggy hair, a striped tunic and...yep, those were breeches.

"I...I..." No other words filtering through her brain connected. He seemed excessively offended at her being in the restricted area. She didn't touch anything. It was only a simple mistake—a medical problem.

"Captain! Captain Price!" the shaggy-haired man hollered. "We have a stowaway!"

At that alarm, men rushed to the unsteady deck and swarmed around her. They gawked like she was either a piece of candy or a filthy criminal. A little excessive for a simple misunderstanding.

Two large hands reached under her arms and lifted her straight off the ladder. "Let me go, you filthy jerks!" Angela swung her legs to free herself, but the men held her just above the deck. "Put me down! I'm not a child."

One released her. The other said with scorn, "Filthy? I resent that, wench."

As she dangled in the air, the gawking men parted for the man in charge. Angela's mouth gaped open. Her sexy pirate taking the inventory was the captain! And in the bright daylight, he was even more handsome and refined. The breeze tousled his hair beneath his hat, and his eyes were a stunning blue like the water. Angela figured she could sweet-talk him out of trouble, and maybe into something else.

"Let her go, Liverman," the captain ordered. Angela swallowed back an audible sigh at his voice, both deep and commanding, but the lilt of the accent stole her breath. Her feet touched the deck, and the men released her arms. She rubbed them with a frown, both for the soreness and the grime.

"You were just below deck, captain," the first shaggy-haired man continued with an accusing tone. "How did you miss a woman below deck?"

The captain assessed her, focusing on her clothing, or what her clothing didn't cover, and amusement lifted his lips just slightly. "Berger, I can certainly assure you I did not miss a woman on board."

Yes, *he did.*

The captain's words were tough, but his gaze said something else entirely—curiosity and amusement. "Certainly not one dressed like that." The captain's head cocked to the side, his gaze raked over her in a different way—steamy and smoldering.

Angela exhaled slowly. The deck listed with a wave, and Angela struck her hands out for balance. The men around her seemed unaffected by the ship's movements, but they had to be used to it. The things she rode had four wheels.

Or two legs.

A man next to her pinched her polyester material with dirty hands. "What is this made of, and why is it so shiny?"

Another man rubbed at the ruffles in her costume. "I don't know, but I think I like it. Less layers to get to the goods underneath." He snickered, and the others whooped with catcalls that made Angela's skin prickle. She twisted, pulling the fabric from their grimy fingers.

When she'd set out to have a good time with Emily, this was not what she'd had in mind. Angela folded her arms in front of her defensively, but with this many animals, any effort to protect herself would be in vain. She craned her neck, trying to see where the dock was, and the deck tilted. A wave splashed and soaked everyone on the main deck. With the force, Angela lost her balance and fell right into the captain's wet arms.

Beyond the blowing salty sea air, a masculine spiciness tickled her nose, and in that instant, the rest of the ship and all her cares and worries melted away. Water dribbled off the rim of his hat. Up close, his eyes were beautiful. His chest was firm, strong against the listing, an anchor, exactly the kind of man she'd been hunting for. Someone with the strength to handle her.

Unfortunately, the scowl on his face meant he didn't reciprocate. "You have caused me quite the problem," the captain growled. "And your timing couldn't have been worse." The captain gripped her arms, stepped back, and released her at a short distance, after assuring himself she was stable on her feet.

"Karl!" the captain shouted. "Send your men up to furl the mizzens."

A barrel-chested man with a bald head nodded and gestured. Slender men rushed up the ratlines in obedience.

The shaggy cretin, Berger, if she remembered right, said, "Stowin' away is cause for marooning, captain. We shan't make exceptions."

Angela swiped dripping hair out of her face, wishing she'd taken her hat from the hold, and folded her arms over her chilled chest. "Marooning? Stowing away? You people can't be serious. I didn't sign up for a reenactment, but if that's the case, take me back to shore, and I'll be going home."

The captain studied her with the same confusion haunting her and the crew. Men around her glanced at each other. Some murmured. A couple lifted their hats and scratched their sweaty, unwashed heads.

"Reenactment?" one whispered to another. "Buckley, you heard of a reenactment?"

A lean man with a leathery face and black shoulder-length hair shrugged and said, "Nay. Where's this pretty creature from?"

Angela chuckled, amused but on the edge of frustration. "Okay, that's enough. I want to go home. Emily! Emily Porter!" she called for her missing friend. No response returned, of course. She faced the men. "It's not funny anymore! Take me home."

Another man, younger than many others, pushed through and said, "What's all the hubbub?" His eyes landed on her and face became bleak. "Oh."

The captain stood before her, white as a fresh winter's snow and speechless.

5

Chapter 5

THE BREWING STORM ROCKED the hull, and they were headed straight through it into enemy territory. Rather than focusing on the brutal task ahead, the men were fretting over the sudden appearance of a woman. They had questions, and he couldn't blame them. Because, despite the chaos, Captain Henry Price stared dumbfounded at her. She was like nothing he'd ever seen before, but two things were familiar. Her accent matched a woman he'd met recently, and he knew the name she called.

Where were these women from?

The quartermaster, Noah Riley, gripped his shoulder against the onslaught of the next wave. "Captain, we must find a port, any port, to shelter against the incoming squall. By Hodgens's calculations, Cuba is the nearest hard, but I think taking our chances against the storm is wiser."

Price only stared at the woman—her bountiful breasts and tantalizing hips. Her arms were thick with muscle and power—not a dainty flower to be damaged by the wind. He'd never been so transfixed, so distracted, in the face of grim danger.

Riley leaned in close, "What's gotten into you, captain? We don't have time to deal with this right now." He glanced at the stowaway and back. Riley was right. They didn't have the time, but Price couldn't ignore the situation either. He'd put out flames over and over when they'd last had a woman on board, and they hadn't known she was a woman at the time. This was so much worse and couldn't have come at a more terrible time.

Liverman, a new member of the rigging crew, leaned closer to her accusingly. "How'd you get aboard? Price, you checked the hold but didn't see her?"

The dark tone ripped Price from his perplexity. "I counted the inventory, and this woman was not there, I assure you." He would've remembered someone so...unusual, completely stunning. His eyes raked over her body and her indescribable outfit once more. Frustrated with himself and this new distraction, Price rubbed his face. He had a tight schedule, a plan, and this turn of events threatened everything he worked toward for months.

"Well then. A sneaky little mouse slipped by all of us and the captain. I wonder what other skills she has," Berger said with a devious glint in his eye.

The newest recruits—some far younger than Price's years—hadn't seen port in two weeks and a prize in longer. A woman in their midst meant belligerence was inevitable, and he needed cooperation to complete the mission at hand. But the rules were the rules.

"Berger, several barrels were unsealed, and this storm threatens our stores. Seal them, would you?" the captain ordered.

Berger grumbled to himself and headed off. That left Liverman, but the captain didn't have any repairs needed to the skeleton of the ship...yet.

"Rules state what happens to the wench, but I'm curious what the captain has in mind." Liverman folded his arms over his soaked chest. "Tell him, Riley."

The quartermaster sent a pleading look to the captain. Riley hadn't encountered such a thing before, and for the first time, the young man was silent.

"Rules?" the woman said with disbelief, interrupting Price's thoughts. "I don't know what's going on here, but I want to be left off this ship." Her features twisted with honest confusion. She was his age, if he wasn't mistaken. "You people are insane. This isn't what I signed up for."

"You didn't sign, wench," Liverman said. "That's the problem."

"I'm not a wench. My name is Angela, and I just want to find my friend and go home." Anger and frustration boiled over her, and she spun, seeking a sympathetic ear among these bilge rats. Most of these men wouldn't budge on the rules. Hell, weeks ago, Price wouldn't have either.

Liverman cackled and pressed a hand on top of his hat to hedge against the gust of wind. "The woman picked her punishment. Marooning! That saves us time."

"Can you not talk about me like I'm not standing in front of you?" Angela asked, anger seething beneath her skin.

Liverman cocked a brow at her, seemingly not understanding the issue, and Price admired her strength to stand up to these men. Perhaps she simply wasn't aware of the level of danger they represented.

Vallo pushed forward. A short man with dark hair, he was quiet and easily ignored. Not seen. Price held him close in esteem, and when the man talked, Price listened. He knew things the crew held from the captain. "Women ain't allowed on this ship. We signed the rules. All of us, and she needs to go!"

Several of the crew cheered their accord. Price shot a dark look at Vallo for rousing the men further. But vocalizing his dissent only strengthened Vallo's position in the crew. Price needed Vallo to maintain their trust.

"We did sign," Price agreed. "But these are special circumstances, which warrant special attention, and since we're facing down a squall, the storm takes precedence."

"Special?" Liverman spat. "Are we tossing out rules when convenient? If that's the case, I know a few that can heave overboard." Liverman stared down the captain, a blatant threat. Oh, how Price hated that man.

"Stand down," Riley warned. "The captain makes the final decision. *That* is also in the rules."

Liverman pinched his face as if catching a whiff of the bilge water, and he folded his arms over his chest, silently waiting for the next declaration to argue.

"Final decision?" Angela blurted, quite ill-mannered. "I'm not a child. I have just as much bearing in this *decision* as you do. I didn't choose this. Bring me back to a nearby city, and I'll be out of your way." With a list of the ship, Angela gripped a line running overhead. It wasn't safe for her to remain out here.

The previous captain, Lemoine, had pulled Price aside and explained his plan to disembark at Nassau permanently and chase after the woman who'd stowed away. At the time, Price believed the captain to be suffering ill humors to drop everything, but when Lemoine explained where the woman came from, Price had worried for the mental state of his esteemed captain. A part of him had been grateful Lemoine retired, for the crew's sake as much as his own.

But now Price was trapped in a conundrum. Had the captain been telling the truth? He was certain no woman hid below deck, and considering her healthful condition, she couldn't have been pilfering provisions from the crew during the weeks since their last port of call. If this incredible magic were indeed real, for her own safety in this foreign world, Price could never allow her to chase after the missing friend all alone, but he also needed the woman off the *Sea Lion*.

His own conscience couldn't send her away nor keep her.

A wave breached the main deck, spraying the crew and soaking the woman again. Her mouth opened in a round shape, once again distracting Price.

Storm clouds closed the distance; the ocean warned them away. Navigating the squall would take all hands and all attention. He couldn't maroon her in this weather—not for the ship's safety or the rowing crew's. But the ship's crew crowded around her like she was a novelty toy.

His decision was made.

"Cantu, bring Angela to my chambers."

Cantu, a docile and dependable man of many talents, including his enormous strength, gripped the woman by the bare arm. Saltwater glistened against her smooth skin, which was the last thing Price needed to be noticing, no matter how long had passed since he felt the warmth of a woman's touch.

"This is an outrage!" Liverman protested.

Price really hated that man.

"I'm not your prisoner! What is this? Unhand me!" Angela struggled futilely in the broad man's grip.

"Captain!" Vallo added.

Price nodded to Cantu, and his trustworthy man ushered her across the deck to the navigation room and into his chamber door under an onslaught of angry protests. Price smiled at her feistiness, but his short-lived amusement was stolen by Liverman.

"Captain?" Liverman said. "We demand an explanation."

Price's patience for the insubordination was gone. They had a squall to best. "See yourself below deck and do your job, otherwise we'll all be at the bottom of the Caribbean Sea."

Cantu returned and gave a nod, indicating the order had been carried out. Price barked out the rest of his orders. "Buckley, batten down the hatches. Cantu, tar the leaks below deck. Vallo"—Price pointed skyward—"furl the lower courses. This storm is unavoidable now. No matter the circumstances, preserve the mainmast! All hands, man your positions!"

The crew sprang into action, and Price ran to the assistance of the helmsman, holding the rudder steady against the onslaught of the ocean's fury. Only a miracle would keep them alive with a ship-swallowing squall upon them, but his mind wandered into his private chamber.

6

Chapter 6

THE SHIP LISTED STARBOARD and port, the waves thrashing and fighting to sink the lumbering trespasser. Angela noticed the parallel. She was a trespasser to these prehistoric animals. Rather than return to the deck and demand her rights with waves attempting to wash them all overboard, Angela braced herself in the cabin. With the desk and bed frame mounted to the floor, the safest place was under the bed. She spread out for stability and gripped two frame legs with all her might.

Angry clouds darkened the skies, dimming the cabin around her. Books fell from the shelves. Silverware clattered to the floorboards and slid. Glass bottles tipped over and some shattered, sending shards bouncing. Cargo nets full of supplies thumped against the wall. Where the angry sea breached the cabin, water trickled from above, soaking the floor.

Soaking Angela.

When Angela had agreed to accompany Emily to the Tall Ships festival and board a tour cruise, she'd expected a romantic sail on the lake under the glittering sun while sidling up next to a handsome man.

This reenactment hadn't been explicitly described on the flier, and had she checked radar, she would've opted out.

On a normal day, Angela loved to control heavy equipment, but even the roughest terrain of her favorite ATV trail had nothing on this old ship and an angry sea. Angela's stomach flipped and sloshed.

One thing was certain, when she returned to the festival grounds, she was going to find the manager and demand a refund—no matter how catty it sounded. And if he wasn't there? A firmly written letter should suffice. Perhaps a complaint on social media as well, but Angela preferred to avoid the tech space.

Her outfit was soaked and torn. Her phone was probably ruined. This was ridiculous.

A leather-bound book slid across the floor and stopped within reach. To give her fatigued arms a break, Angela scooted backward under the bed and braced her legs against the frame. She reached out for the book to keep her mind off her stomach. Maybe she could find a refund allowance, or a free parking pass, or something about the company she could use to alleviate her aggravation and inconvenience.

Angela flipped opened the cover and her lips parted. Loopy, angled handwriting—like something from a history museum—delicately penned on pale yellow pages. Fascinated, she deciphered the penmanship, what little of it she could. This was the captain's log.

They wouldn't put a prop in here, out of view of the paying public, would they?

Angela turned the moist page. In orderly columns, locations and dates detailed inventory on and off the ship. Several lines down, she read, "Goats and pigs. What in the world...?"

More paragraphs detailed weather events and ships encountered both at port and on the sea. Angela turned the page, unable to resist the book's allure. The crew's names and dollar amounts were listed—some were only ten and twenty bucks. Angela's face pulled into a frown. "Well, add that to my list of complaints. If the company paid better, they'd probably treat their guests better."

The groaning ship leveled, and Angela relaxed her legs and climbed out from under the bed. The cabin was a mess, and she was filthy. Testing the mattress and finding it soaked, Angela stayed on her feet while sweeping water and dirt off her arms and legs. Finally, this horrible chaos was over. Now she could disembark and fly home.

Shouts from the deck were muffled by the cabin. The ship stopped with an abrupt shudder, sending Angela careening over onto her knees. A loud crack—she was certain wasn't her own bones—turned her head. Angela frowned at the closed cabin door while standing up and brushing off yet again. Did they hit the dock at port? With the way those men treated her, she wouldn't doubt their ability to do their jobs.

Shouts permeated the wood. The water clinging to every surface of the cabin was warm enough to not worry her, but it was too cool for comfort. Gooseflesh rose on her arms.

Something was wrong.

The starboard side of the ship listed severely. The book slid along the floor, sticking against broken glass. Angela tumbled across the cabin and slammed into the wall with a sharp pain to her hip. Water poured in from all the seams in the walls. The ship wasn't righting itself, and instead of the water draining out to the lower decks, it was filling the cabin. Water reached her ankles and then knees way too fast.

Something was very wrong.

Angela climbed toward the door, pulled it open, and braced herself against the wall. Some sort of navigation room. Instruments clattered to the floor. The ship tilted further. No matter the captain's orders or the crew's baser desires, she had to get out of here. With the alarming angle, the door to the navigation room fell open and more seawater rushed in like a waterfall. Angela climbed toward the door, fighting the thigh-deep current throwing her back toward the captain's quarters—now nearly submerged.

Heart pounding her chest, Angela tried to swim toward the exit. Men were jumping over the rail. Others were splashing in the water as if they couldn't swim.

A hand reached into the doorframe, fingers splayed. The captain's head popped into view with panic on his handsome face. He braced himself. "The ship's going down! Give me your hand!"

Her rescuer was unstable too with the water pushing him, spraying around his body. If he lost his grip, they were both going to drown. Angela's breathing became shallow, and she fought to move her legs against the current, but she couldn't. She dove into the water to swim toward the captain's hand, but still the current was too strong, throwing her back against the wall. Angela considered herself a good swimmer, on an ordinary day, but being trapped in a small room rapidly filling with water deteriorated her self-confidence. Fear constricted her chest, and exertion burned her legs. If she didn't get out, she would die.

Another loud crack pierced her eardrum. The captain looked over his shoulder, eyes wide with concern.

"Now!" he shouted to her.

Using gaps between the wood boards of the wall, Angela climbed toward him, and when in reach, she grabbed his hand, her safety line. His grip was firm, sticky from the saltwater, and reassuring that he would bring them to safety. The captain gritted his teeth and with a grunting force, pulled her through the door just as the water overtook the opening. Suction pulled her back toward the door, but the captain held on.

Several feet of water covered the main deck. Rain pummeled the surface, blinding her. Thunder rumbled overhead. As the bow raised in the air, the stern beneath her feet sunk further, and Angela treaded water.

The captain's hand was torn from her. He hadn't surfaced.

Only a few men splashed in desperation around the ship. One clung to the top of the mainmast, still exposed to the storm's elements. Where was everyone else? Where was the captain?

Angela turned herself to find him, but a wave crashed overhead, pushing her down into the murky depths. She kicked and thrashed, fighting against the force of the ocean and the pull of the sinking ship. As the wave rolled by, the suction lessened, and Angela's efforts inched her closer to the air.

Debris in the water clouded her vision—loose ropes, pieces of wood, and other objects she didn't recognize. A broken chunk of wood floated up next to her, and she grabbed it. The board helped her kick, propelling her upward. Her face broke the surface, and Angela gasped and coughed. She kept her chest pressed against the board like a life preserver.

Smaller waves blocked her view of the destruction around her. The ship had broken on a rocky outcropping, but the island cliff was too steep to climb. Angela kicked away from the rocks before getting tossed against them herself.

"Captain!" Angela shouted, but the departing storm muffled her voice. She kicked and paddled, hoping to find a suitable place to climb onto land. She rode the shorter waves, and a gasp nearby turned her head.

There! Captain Price's face breached the surface, and with a deep breath, he slipped below. Angela paddled over as quickly as possible, fighting the current trying to throw her into the rocks. She craned her neck, trying to find him. She was sure he was last right here.

He was gone.

Angela shoved a hand down and, fingers splayed, tried to reach him. Still nothing.

The man tried to keep her safe from his unruly crew. And if the storm was going to take her life, she didn't want to be alone at the end. Releasing the board, she dove under the surface.

The captain wasn't far away, but he was sinking. The man fought to remove the heavy garments pulling him down. With desperation, Angela reached him and helped remove his coat and boots. With all her might, she pushed him upward and kicked wildly to catch up to him.

His foot tangled on a sinking nest of ropes. Angela shifted the heavy hemp off his foot and continued to climb the water stroke after stroke. Her mouth broke the surface, and she gasped. The captain breached next to her, gasping and coughing.

Through the pummeling rains, her life preserving board floated nearby. She paddled over to it and brought it back to him. The captain gripped it, panting.

"Good to know you can swim," he said, managing a smile.

Angela snorted. "Good to know you can sail." If Angela had been steering the ship—after getting lessons on how to do it—she was certain it wouldn't have crashed against the rocks.

The captain cocked his weary head at her in amusement.

"If we stay here, we're going to die of exhaustion trying to stay ahead of those rocks. Paddle with me."

The captain mirrored her on the board, elbow to elbow. They squinted into the torrential rains, and together they kicked through the angry water, keeping an eye out for other survivors.

"I don't see anyone else." Angela swiped ocean spray from her face, thankful the thunderous storm had moved on.

"Most of them can't swim." The captain cleared his face and coughed on water trapped in his lungs. "But I'm fortunate you can."

After rigorous thrashing, they made headway around a corner. The cove was dense forest with a strip of beach rimming it. Debris from the ship tickled the shore. A few men rested with the water licking at their soggy boots.

"Over there. Stop over by those men," Captain Price said.

Angela changed trajectory, and together they paddled until their toes touched sand, waters calmer by the protective cove. Rain pattered the trees.

The captain dragged the board on shore, and Angela fell into the sand herself, laying face up and panting. Working hard in the warehouse during the peak of summer, hitting three figures in temperature, was nothing compared to that, and it was something she never wanted to experience again.

Writing a letter to festival management seemed so...insufficient...now, and far too much work. The rain softened, and slowly the darker clouds floated away, dragging in white clouds. Angela blinked against the rainfall, but her body wouldn't move.

Every summer she'd spend weekends with Emily, drinking on the beach, watching the clouds drift by, picking out the shapes. They'd hammer the stakes and pitch their tent, cut firewood, and light it—with lighter fluid. They weren't Lewis and Clark reincarnated. Right now, Angela didn't have the energy for any of that. Right now, nature's cozy blanket or endless fury would decide how she spent the night.

She faded into a deep sleep with one question on her mind: where was Emily?

7

Chapter 7

SHE'D SAID, 'GOOD TO *know you can sail.*' It should've been an insult, but with the friendly tone she'd used, Price could only chuckle at the irony. He was a fantastic sailor, but he'd replayed the events over and over, trying to determine if there was something that could've prevented such a catastrophe. Should he have ordered reefing sooner? Had they not heaved-to quickly enough? Had the drogue not been deployed on time?

During the night on the beach in soaked clothing with sand in places it didn't belong, Price decided his preoccupation with Angela had caused the ship's wreck. If he and the crew hadn't been distracted, they could've maneuvered safely through the squall. Instead, the ship had been dashed against a crag. His plan included having a ship, and not only had he suffered that loss, but now he didn't know how many of his crew remained. Angela remained, and she was still turning his life upside down. Price's sleep had been terrible, all because he'd kept an eye on her, sleeping soundly as a rock all night.

Daylight broke on the horizon, magnified by the ocean's reflection, beaming bright light into his eyes. Price groaned and rolled over onto his sore hip. Every muscle in his body ached. His fingers were stiff from gripping the helm with

Hodgens and fighting to keep the *Sea Lion* afloat. All for naught, and time had never been a luxury to waste.

Price sighed and grunted as he stood, bare toes sinking into the sand. He looked down at the curious sensation. When he'd been descending beneath the ocean's surface, hope truly lost but before panic set in, Angela had removed his boots and helped him shuck his coat. If not for her, he'd have drowned. Among his crew, less than a dozen could've done the same for him, and still, none did. Price would never forget an action so bold, so courageous and noble. He knew of only one person in his life worthy of such similar description—William Price—but the man had perished for his efforts. Captain Price couldn't let another meet that fate.

At low tide, the beach had grown significantly in size. Angela was still asleep, and his crew had already set to work. With so many questions invading his thoughts, Price left her, strolling along the beach, checking the flotsam for salvage or even a pair of boots. Along the way to the scene of the wreck, he collected an armful of spare lines and an empty barrel, but he dropped them with a gaped mouth at the *Sea Lion*'s condition. The damage before him twisted his insides. The vengeful sea had deposited the ship next to the rocky outcrop with a fatal gaping maw in her hull. Like visiting a gravesite, his ship was gone.

With stiff knees, Captain Price approached, and near the keel, a fallen sailor rocked in the softly lapping waves. Hayes. A fair man. Price considered whether the man's feet were of similar size before shaking his head at the loss and moving on.

Quartermaster Noah Riley ducked out of the hole and stretched. Upon sighting him, the younger man exclaimed, "Captain, you survived!" Riley embraced him with a pat on the back and obvious relief. Becoming captain was not a position to take lightly, and Riley wouldn't have wanted it thrust upon him.

Price pulled back with a grin. "I had help. I'm surprised to have found you upright and breathing. You swim as well as a line tied to an anchor. Remember when you fell overboard?"

Riley struggled to recount the tale, and the moment he did was evident on his face. "A gale heeled the ship, and I tumbled leeward over the rail. I floundered, but a rescue line luckily landed in my hands. I had different luck this time." Riley wiped his brow. "A tight stay can be the difference between sailing the seas and paying an eternal visit to the depths below."

The sound of lapping waves reminded him of the lost souls, and Price's levity left him on a breath. "What of the others? How many men do we have left?"

"About two dozen. In your absence, I had Giles set up a camp just inside the cove, hidden in the jungle, and I've rallied a few men to salvage what we can. McKee volunteered to collect, wrap, and record the bodies. I didn't argue, since we no longer have a doctor on board. Among the casualties are Miller and Cruz, and clearly Hayes. But a fair warning, Liverman, Vallo, and Berger survived. Berger clung to the mizzenmast not far from me. We have much damage to repair on the ship and families to recompense, I don't believe our reserve is sufficient."

Just when Price thought he'd received all the bad news, the men agitating the crew were going to continue their quarrel.

With no doctor, the duties fell to the carpenter, and without a carpenter, the remaining crew—and Price himself—would find themselves in yet worse dire straits. "What of the ship's repair? Where's Buckley?"

"Buckley is with Cantu in the hold, removing what cargo and personal effects of value remain, and determining the tools and supplies available for repair. Peter Gunner is assessing the guns and salvageable shot. Karl Dillon needs more hands to refit the lines on deck, but Liverman is up there helping. Berger is refilling our water barrels, what of them remains. But even if we can bring the *Sea Lion* to rights, I'm uncertain whether we have sufficient hands to sail her."

If that didn't burst his remaining bubble of positivity, he didn't know what would.

"You've done well, Riley."

"Captain, I don't know if you've noticed, but we're stranded on Cuba. If the enemy catches wind of our location and current state, we won't need to worry about having hands to sail," Riley said in confidence.

Price gritted his teeth. Unbeknownst to the crew, Price had planned to sail this way, but their landing here too soon was entirely accidental, and with their ship hobbled, not at all convenient. Before the crew voted Henry Price as quartermaster and, subsequently, captain, he and his older brother, William, were English Royal Navy, sailing with the HMS Bristol. Several years ago, pirate Ernest Wilcox of the *Sea Lion* captured the Bristol, a brazen move by any standards. But after being pressed, Henry and William accepted their freedom with open arms and relished in assisting other crews to their own freedoms—while filling their coffers in the process. Henry had sailed with William for years, and both of them planned to become captains of their own ships and sail together as a flotilla.

But it wasn't to be.

And the guilt Henry Price had carried festered, until it became rage—a silent, patient being, growing and maturing the perfect plan to exact that vengeance. But with every passing hour, the tide was returning to claim her prize. With every passing hour, the risk of being spotted by Spain increased tenfold. And Riley was right.

"I'm very aware of our location. Keep everyone quiet while we work. No shanties, no shouting. Are we clear?"

Riley nodded. "One last thing, captain. What of the woman?"

Seemed Riley couldn't forget her either, and at the thought of that special woman resting in the sand, Price bit back a smile. "She's sleeping in the cove."

Riley grinned. "I don't suppose, since we're no longer on the ship in a technical manner, the articles shall allow those of us wanting to take a turn?"

Images of the crew lined up, one by one, stealing her virtue while she helplessly screamed, fighting and failing to stop them, assaulted his brain. Price's sore hands curved into solid fists. Since she'd saved his life, he would protect her until she released him of the duty. It was the least he could do.

Through gritted teeth and a tense jaw, Price said, "Regardless of the status of our ship, we are still on the account, so the articles are still in force. She is not to be disturbed. If any men care to voice an opinion on the matter, send for me. Conveniently, we happen to be on shore to settle disputes."

Riley's smile slid away, but he stood firm in his position. "Your point is understood, and I shall direct opposition to you, but the articles also state any woman caught on board are to suffer death."

Price stepped forward. "If any of the crew insists on marooning her or any similar punishments while the ship remains a husk on the exposed sandbar, I wish to address them immediately. The woman is not their concern. We need the *Sea Lion* back on the water."

"Captain, she broke the articles. If you refuse them the rights in the articles, the crew will insist on reparations, and if the woman isn't from a wealthy family, they just might insist on receiving their payment in another form. And then we circle back to the original question."

If Riley pushed for using the woman one more time... "You have my answer. Go."

The quartermaster smiled in a friendly way, returning to the carefree young man Price knew so well. Riley swatted him on the shoulder. "I agree with you entirely. I only wanted to prepare you for the crew's opinion. I know how close Lemoine was to losing their trust, and I don't want to see this strange woman destroy everything you've built here."

"I appreciate the sentiment," Price said dryly, the hypothetical status of the conversation not having sunk in. Price climbed up to the tilted deck, not looking forward to Liverman's judgment. Only a few men were up here, including his boatswain, Karl Dillon. Liverman was busy on the other side, and Price joined a pair about to run the rigging through a replacement pulley.

Riley's words plagued him. Could one woman's presence dismantle everything Price had been planning?

"'Alo, captain, glad to see another set of hands." Peter Gunner twisted lines into an expert knot. He was a poorly named gunner's mate. The boy could repair weapons with the best of them, but his aim was something terrible. The kid had heart though. No surprise master gunner, McKee, had directed Peter onto the main deck. "Secure!"

"Pull!" Price yelled, and the men coordinated their efforts. "Pull!" Price repeated and gritted his teeth, heaving with all his might. The wood of the ship creaked in protest, threatening to snap, but it was a necessary risk.

"Steady!" Boatswain Karl Dillon yelled.

Price held firm with Peter at his side. The rigging was a snarled mess all over the deck and sand. How were they going to fix this by the return of the tide tonight?

While Price held steady with all his might, Karl lashed the ropes around the rocky outcrop and gestured for them to let go. "She's stable, but not for long."

The captain released his grip. "Good work, men! Let's get her capturing wind again."

The handful of men cheered quietly while they continued working. Most of his crew were agreeable—men he trusted to cooperate on their shared goal. Since they'd sacrificed so much just to reach this island, how would they react when they discovered his personal objective now?

Cantu approached down the beach, carrying a heavy log on his shoulder, and he gestured for the captain's attention.

Price climbed down the outer hull, landing his bare feet in the sand.

"Captain, the woman's awake."

"Is she distressed in any way?"

Cantu shook his thick head. "More like a scared bilge rat. Reminds me of my little sister in a way, except for the unusual garments."

Price's lips pressed thin at the mention of her clothing. Why she had any effect on him at all was confusing. Their sole relationship was a favor for a favor—and she wasn't aware of the arrangement yet. "Never mind her dress. I'll handle the woman."

8
Chapter 8

ANGELA STARED AT THE sand around her and absorbed its cool, damp touch. She turned her hands over and marveled at the white grains. With a finger, she pushed grains off, a swipe here and another swipe, and they sprinkled onto her lap.

Angela unzipped the pack at her waist and groaned. Her credit cards were full of sand. The ink on her club cards ran, and the paper disintegrated. Everything was ruined. She took out her cell phone, but even if for some reason a cell tower existed, her battery was dead. Or the saltwater ate it.

It felt real.

Wisconsin didn't have palm trees or oppressive humidity. There wasn't any minty colored saltwater. Wisconsin's beaches weren't white. She hadn't flown anywhere, and she was certain she didn't drive across the USA and wander without supplies into the jungle. She loved camping, but she wasn't reckless. Her skimpy pirate wench outfit, which she put on while standing in her apartment, was still on her body—now torn, crispy with the evaporated water, and scratchy with sand. But just as all this was clear, so was a sinking ship and saving the captain's life.

That felt real, but it couldn't be.

Years after Angela had been cast aside by both her families, Mom's replacement family struggled to deal with her new behaviors and begged Angela for help. Angela's mother had woven unbelievable tales of adventures she'd had during the night, and when Angela insisted they were just dreams, her mom lashed out. Then the sleep walking and blackouts started. The arguments over her safety morphed into fights.

After visits with specialists, Mom was diagnosed with dementia, and the blackouts and wild tales increased. Angela reluctantly toured skilled nursing facilities, dreading every step because Mom was too young for this. But her new family didn't have the emotional space or time to dedicate to her rapidly deteriorating condition. They couldn't keep her safe. Each facility was worse than the next, and Angela didn't have the heart to leave her mother in one. Angela offered to take Mom in, wanting to finally connect for the first time in years, to pick up where they'd left off and pretend the last two decades hadn't happened. A few days before she was ready to move in, Mom had an accident. And once again her mom had left her.

Please let this be real.

Angela could handle almost anything, but losing her mind scared her the most. Grains of sand glinted against the sunlight, and Angela shifted her legs just enough to catch the light and marvel at the sparkles.

The sparkles are real.

The sparkles are real.

The sparkles are real. Oh, please, be real.

DOWN IN THE COVE, Angela sat upright on the beach, right where he'd left her. After yesterday and last night, she must've been exhausted. As they all were, but they had a long day ahead of them. Extra long for Captain Price. With the crew moving along in their duties, but no imminent danger, they'd be calling for an answer. Price didn't have a satisfactory one to offer. As he closed the distance between them, Berger emerged from the jungle with an empty barrel and approached her.

Price broke into a jog on the soggy sand and reached her before anything serious happened.

"I knew it's bad luck to have a woman on board." Berger stood at her feet and spat on the sand. "Look at what you gone and done. You need to pay for all the damage you caused, woman."

Riley's assumption for the crew wanting Angela to work off her debts was dreadfully accurate. Price slowed his steps. "That's enough, Berger. Get back to work."

Berger spun on him. "And you, captain, steering us straight into Spain's territory like you have a wish for death. Liverman is right about you." With an angry glare, the shaggy-haired ingrate strolled down the beach with the barrel over a shoulder and spat into the water.

Price kept an eye on him until the man disappeared around the corner of the cove. Satisfied, Price sat on the sand next to her. "My apologies for him. The men aren't accustomed to women on board. In fact, it's against the rules."

Angela brushed sand off her hands, glassy eyes concentrating on her sandy legs, which Price found himself admiring. "Rules? A shipwreck and misogyny in my dreams. What'll I think up next?" Angela said with disbelief.

Price wasn't sure what that meant. "I owe you a great debt of gratitude, but at this moment, I find myself wondering the correct path I must take with you."

As if awakened from a daydream, Angela met his gaze and frowned. "What does that mean?"

"We have much more pressing concerns right now, but the crew is unsettled. They will want some satisfaction, and answering for a stowaway is how I can reunite the crew when I need them most focused."

"I'm not a stowaway. I don't know how I got on that ship."

Price believed her. "No boy or woman to be allowed amongst us. Any found are to suffer death," Price recited. "It's an agreement we all signed. It prevents distractions and disgruntlement among the crew. And as you can see, your presence is causing precisely that. The quartermaster will have no choice but to ensure the rules are followed."

"Death?" Angela said with a pinch of disgust. "Isn't almost dying good enough punishment to them?"

"I'm afraid not." It was good enough for Price, though.

"Look at me!" Angela said, flinging her arms up in the air. "My cheap costume in a bag is shredded, my credit cards are full of sand and damaged by this sticky salty water. I still have my necklace, but it serves no purpose now. I need clothes, and I need to go home—with Emily. Where's Emily? Was she on that ship? Is she...dead?"

The wildness in her eyes and the rapid rise and fall of her ample chest made Price feel terrible for her state. He touched her hand and spoke softly, "I assure you, no such Emily went down with the ship."

"Then where is she?" Angela asked, terror in her beautiful brown eyes.

Price couldn't explain without risking everyone's safety, and right now he had a bigger problem—a broken ship on enemy territory. He craned his neck to keep watch for movement in the trees. Even if the crew managed to hide all the washed-up debris, the fresh markings on the sand would tell the locals they had company.

"I can help you, if you help me." It shamed him to make that offer, knowing a woman's hand should never have to do a man's labor, but he needed anyone able-bodied to help.

With a frown and a steely gaze, Angela said, "How?"

Price couldn't allow her to wander the hostile island alone—whether she searched for her friend or for a way home. Dealing with the inflexible and sometimes feral crew was still safer, as long as she stayed by Price's side. "That squall crippled our ship, and I lost many good men. If we cannot make repairs posthaste, we shall succumb to the enemy. I know how the crew will react over this. I blame them not; it's their nature. They might even challenge my captaincy, but I'm prepared to take that risk to protect you."

Her face twisted, and she shifted her body away from his. "Protect me? I don't need protection; I need a plane ticket. What is wrong with your company? I'm a customer, a *paying* customer. This reenactment stuff is...exhausting. I'm done. I've had enough. I need a shower. I need to get out of these ridiculous clothes. I have a shift on Monday, and I don't know if I can get home that fast. If I get fired over this..." Angela paused and studied his face. Some of the anger deflated. "You're serious. We're stranded here? Don't you have radios for the Coast Guard or something?"

"I don't understand." Just as he hadn't understood many of Emily Porter's actions and words.

"Explain to me why you can't call the head office for assistance," Angela said.

"If Spain discovers our presence in their territory, they will relish in seeing us swinging at the gallows. No company would move against the state, certainly not for us. There is no assistance out here. We help each other."

Angela snorted. "What company doesn't care about its employees? They have to maintain some liability insurance. You have a way with words that's so unusual. Did they teach you that in some acting school?"

Once again, her words baffled him. But if she questioned the crew in the same manner, she'd find herself with more attention than she'd prefer. Price had to remedy that risk. "It's not a school one learns to speak from. It's how one was raised."

"You were raised in England to speak like some lord duke guy?" Her brow lifted, a bit of amusement returned.

Price understood two of those descriptors. "Indeed...I wager?"

"Your family must be a hoot. I'm sorry." Angela sighed and looked up at the sky. "No reception out here in the middle of nowhere. And...no airports. Fine. What do you want from me?" Angela stood and her sharp heels sunk into the sand. Price attempted to assist her balance, but she crashed over too quickly and fell back onto the sand. Angela ripped off her boots and flung the curious things aside. She rose once again and brushed her dress and legs. "And if you say anything about me wearing less clothing or servicing or laying down or anything remotely like that—you can kiss my ass." Angela paused from her cleaning and looked Price in the eye. "But not literally. You know what I mean. Why can't I have normal dreams?"

Price climbed to his bare feet. Reception in a context that made no sense. Airports... Plane ticket... Reenactment... Radio... Words Price didn't understand. Captain Lemoine had told Price the unbelievable tale of the woman from the future who carried proof on her person. At the time, Price had worried about the mental state of his captain and brushed off such nonsense. But Angela was so different from anything familiar, except her stark similarity to Emily. And Angela's rants about things that couldn't be possible in his worldly travels only confirmed what he'd expected...and feared.

Angela Foxe was from the future, and she believed she was dreaming.

Suddenly curious of her life and everything the future had to offer, Price dared not scare her further. While he wanted to embrace her and reassure her everything would be fine, he couldn't. Price couldn't make that promise, and he didn't think she'd want his comfort. Instead, Price spoke honestly. "I understand how different this is for you, and I offer my apologies."

Angela's beautiful features softened. The urge to stroke her face and feel the softness of her skin under his fingertips was a powerful force he hadn't felt before. He wanted to touch those long dark waves cascading over her shoulders in wild loops.

"Apologies don't get us closer to home."

Something in her hair was curious. Price tilted his head and reached for it. "You seem to have some debris...what was this?" Price took the liberty of pulling a piece of metal from her hair—one side straight and the other lumpy. He pressed the blunt end into his fingertip. "I daresay, this is—"

"It's just a bobby pin." Angela snatched the curious thing from his hand and carelessly stuffed it back into her hair.

Price added that to the list of strange words. "If you help me get the *Sea Lion* back on the water, I promise you safe passage to whatever destination you choose."

"Fine. Time's ticking away, and I can't get fired." Angela marched down the beach, motivated by his promise. A small corner of his mind wished her motivation didn't come from the promise of leaving. But the idea of any other ending was preposterous. She was from a different world than him and keeping her alive would be a test like no other.

Price jogged to catch up, wanting to brace her for the site. McKee had been collecting bodies, and Price wasn't sure if the master gunner had collected Hayes yet. At the edge of the cove, he called, "Wait, I beg of you."

Angela stopped, facing the wreckage beyond the cove. She didn't move. She didn't speak.

9

Chapter 9

The ship, listed on its hull in the sand at low tide, was real as anything she'd seen. The storm, the sinking, that had to have been real. The tour ship with the reenactment crew was real. Angela believed none of that was a dream, but that only reinforced her concerns over her lucidity. Men worked tirelessly to untangle and repair the rigging and mend the sails. A hammer rhythmically pounded, slowly filling the giant hole in the hull. They used rugged hand tools. Salvaged materials. Angela frowned. What kind of modern company made their employees use old scraps for repairs? What company would abandon a ship full of employees? OSHA would have a field day with this.

The sunlight glinted on the water. Birds flew overhead. Just birds. Why hadn't a single plane flown by? Where were the motorboats? Container ships? Jet Skis? Judging by the palm-tree-shaped trees, they were somewhere tropical, which meant tourists should be noisy, littering, something.

A lump at the edge of the water, drifting with the gentle waves, caught her eye. Angela peered, squinting. It was human shaped with torn and stained clothing. It couldn't be... It wasn't... Was it?

"Is that a...?" Angela stepped closer. The pale drawn face with dead eyes made her jump back with a screech. "He's dead? Why hasn't anyone called the authorities? Where's EMS?" She gazed at the man's empty face. Where were the police?

Price stood at her shoulder and followed her gaze. He said softly, "This must be is confusing for you, because I know it is for me."

Angela gazed at him pointedly.

"I don't know what 'EMS' is."

How could he not know who the paramedics were? Angela studied the handsome man next to her. From bare toes and torn breeches to a hand sewn tunic and shaggy head of dark hair matted with sand. "What's the English version of EMS then? You know, paramedics."

Price only shook his head.

Could a poor sailor from England really never have heard of emergency medical services? He'd never seen or heard of a bobby pin either. How was it possible? "Cell phone? Jet Skis? Any of this ringing a bell?"

Price shook his head again.

Angela couldn't believe this. "You aren't from some isolated tribe in the middle of nowhere. You understand society. So how can you have no idea about technology?"

Price lit up. "I do have a few technological advancements." He faced his destroyed ship and his excitement fell. "I had...anyway."

Cautiously, Angela asked, "Like what?"

"Our last prize furnished us with a sextant. The men were ecstatic, as you can imagine. Navigation shall be so much more accurate now..." Price trailed off and looked at her face.

"Navigation? Like GPS?"

"I'm not familiar with that term."

"Global Positioning System. It uses satellites to track your position around the globe. Common for cars and boats to get where they need to go and not get lost." She felt like a jerk trying to school a grown man on basic foundations of society, but she couldn't believe his lack of knowledge.

Price just stared, completely dumbfounded.

There was no way this guy never heard of satellites. None of this made any sense. "So, you're telling me this whole lord duke guy captain persona and the penmanship in the captain's log are real? That ship *isn't* a tourist replica?" Asking the questions made her feel absolutely stupid, but she didn't know how else to bridge this disconnect between them.

"As you can touch me, I am authentic."

Angela knew she wasn't asleep. The lukewarm water and cool sand on her feet told her so. Her mom's hallucinations had always been grounded in reality. Angela's imagination was never this vivid or creative. Was she losing her mind? Or had something truly scientifically impossible occurred?

With a deep exhale, Angela steeled herself for the answer. Hesitantly, she reached out and pinched his fabric between her fingers. It felt real with every fiber of her being. She looked into his gorgeous blue eyes and pressed a palm to his heart. It beat rapidly, just like hers.

Captain Price pressed his hand over hers. Warmth penetrated her skin.

Death for simply being aboard. The men's outrage at her stowing away. No technology. The logbook. "Where am I?" she asked in a gentle whisper.

Price pressed his hand harder as if preparing her. "On the bank of Cuba in the Caribbean Sea."

There was a piece still missing, and she was crazy for asking. "When? What year is it?"

"The year of our lord, 1715."

Angela's knees gave out on her, and Price caught her with his strong grasp. He pulled her into a tight embrace, and she squeezed him back, face nestling at his collarbone. Angela's shoulders gently shook with quiet sobs of relief. None of this was a reenactment in real life or a dream from her uncreative mind.

Time travel was a farce, an impossible, with paradoxes preventing it from ever happening. It wasn't possible whatsoever. So, that meant Angela had to be trapped in a sleep walking hallucination. She was losing her mind, just like her mom. No wonder her mom had been so adamant what she'd seen was real, because this was damned convincing.

It was real to her.

Angela closed her eyes, tightening her squeeze on his collar, relishing his touch, and Price's head rested against hers. He smelled of the sea and masculine sweat. And just as before, he felt like her anchor, like a flannel blanket wrapped snugly in front of a winter cabin's crackling fireplace, or a summer evening with butterflies dancing across the meadow, or an autumn breeze swirling red and yellow leaves across neighborhood lawns with pumpkin spice wafting through the air. He was comforting, relaxing.

After Brandon Spindleton tossed their relationship away like yesterday's news, she'd only wanted a commitment-free good time, never to be heartbroken again. Never to be rejected from her loved ones again. From what she'd seen of the captain, he was a gentleman, considerate and caring when he didn't have to be. The strong arms wrapped around her didn't feel like Brandon's. The soft sand under her feet didn't feel like the Persian rugs of his mother's estate. And yet, Angela pulled away from the captain's embrace, reluctantly, to double check the man before her was not Brandon and that she hadn't just hallucinated everything since the tragic wedding.

Angela rubbed her eyes and nose and looked at him again. Rough, rugged, tanned from hard labor in the sun. The opposite of Brandon. Could she have an affair with a hallucination?

With the way he looked...

Captain Price slipped something out of his pocket, and he held it out to her. "Does this help you?"

She accepted the shiny gold disk and turned it over. A coat of arms was stamped into the rudimentary coin. On the flip side were a series of letters and symbols. Nothing like anything she was familiar with. "It's not Lady Liberty."

"It's a Spanish piece of eight. This one was recovered from the treasure fleet that departed from this very island and wrecked near Florida a few weeks past."

Angela handed it back. She remembered Emily had mentioned something about a bunch of gold lost off the Florida coast, much of which had never been recovered. Angela was only half listening. History never interested her. She was paying attention now. This wasn't salvaged after centuries of sea water exposure. This was new. "You're certain that's the source of this coin?"

"Positively. I was there collecting it."

Angela blinked. She wasn't hallucinating either. She wasn't suffering from an early onset of her mom's disease. Then how the hell had she gone back in time? It simply wasn't possible. What was in the past didn't matter. The bigger concern was how was she going to get home? There were no cabs, no flights, no GPS, no phones....

On her wedding day, in head-to-toe exquisite chiffon and organza, Angela held her phone with an image that shattered her life. She remembered exactly what she'd thought at the time. Angela cackled.

"What is it?" Price asked gently.

"I wished I never saw another phone again in my life. When they say to be careful what you wish for, they mean it."

"Who's they?"

"I don't know." Angela studied his curious face. "Why didn't you ask me what a phone was, or GPS, or any of the other things I mentioned?"

Price shifted his weight and returned his attention to the ship, deflecting her question. "It matters not. We have a tide returning and a ship to fix. Are you up to the task?"

With terrible timing, Angela's stomach growled. She hadn't eaten since yesterday. Captain Price glanced at her, having heard it too, and he held out his arm like a gentleman. Angela embraced it, if for no other reason than she wanted to touch him, to keep herself grounded in this unbelievable reality. But instead of bringing her toward the ship, he brought her to the mouth of the cove. Just inside the dense vegetation, a hefty fellow had collected a circle of rocks, and above it, he'd whittled a spit.

Price dug in his pocket again and offered that same gold coin. "Giles, see if this will fetch a pig. Be discreet about it."

Giles the cook stood up and beamed, taking the coin. "Oh, this is plenty. Thank you, captain."

"Giles," the captain called after him, "see if you can find a set of clothing for the lady."

"And a set of boots for you both?"

Price nodded, and Giles headed out to shop.

"With that settled, we can get to work," Price said to her.

That piece, belonging in museum, was accepted currency, worth the cost of clothing and a pig at least. Angela had no concept of how valuable it really was. This world was fascinating, but as much as she loved to camp with Emily, Angela had her limits on the wildlife. She wanted to go home, and the longer they lingered, the longer it took. "What do you need me to do?"

The captain assessed the ship. "Can you wield a hammer?"

Angela smiled. "Finally, something I understand."

THE JAGGED HOLE IN the hull stood out like an eerie cavern warning them away. The scrawny man named Buckley, in desperate need of a barber, hammered mismatched pieces of wood into the gap, and Cantu, the size of a bulldozer, painted something black on the hull. Others were up in the ratlines, untangling and refastening the rigging, shouting orders to each other.

The quartermaster approached her and the captain with a broad smile, carrying a hammer. Angela figured him for the type of guy to be annoyingly happy in every circumstance, but considering where she stood, she'd take a little optimism.

"Status update, Riley? Where are we at?" Captain Price asked.

"Much of the hold is intact, but we lost all the tobacco and sugar, and we need a new cat."

"Cat?" Angela asked. Emily had said something about a cat being used to whip people as a punishment.

"Cantu says the little bugger scurried up the island shortly after the wreck. Damn resilient things, aren't they? But they're excellent mousers," Riley clarified.

Oh, he meant a real cat.

"If it were up to me, captain," the quartermaster continued, "we'd make all sign-ups and presses swim a quarter league. Our turnover rate would be much lower, I'd wager."

"Thank you for your council, Riley. I found us another hand to help." Price gestured at her.

Riley assessed Angela and frowned. She was used to working in a man-centric world, and she could handle what they threw at her, but she had to be careful in this barbarous world. If they threatened her, there was no police to come rescue her.

Quartermaster Riley shifted his body weight. "Captain, are you sure that's a wise idea?"

"We've discussed this already," Captain Price said.

"We have not discussed her joining our crew."

"She's only helping. There's nothing in the articles about helping."

"She's a woman," Riley said with a set jaw.

Seriously, this guy was insufferable. Being a woman didn't mean she was incapable. "I can help as well as any man."

The quartermaster's brows lifted. "Is that so?"

Angela nodded.

"Then you believe you can handle an angry pile of sailors?"

Concerned he meant what she was afraid he meant, Angela asked, "Handle them *how*?"

Riley leaned in close. "Prevent them from"—his eyes raked down her chest—"releasing...tension."

Angela snatched the hammer from his grip and leveled it on her shoulder like a baseball bat. She growled out, "Just try it. I dare you."

Riley backed up with palms open and brows lifted. "Message received." He turned to the captain. "I warned you. Whatever happens is your responsibility."

"Get back to work."

With a final glare, the quartermaster left.

"What did he warn you about?" she asked.

"It's been handled." The captain led her closer to the ship and shouted into the hull's hole, "Buckley!"

A general call of acknowledgment came from inside the hole.

Price added, "Need a hand?"

The lean man with a leathery face and black shoulder-length hair from the deck, who'd called her pretty, popped out of the hole. He grinned, displaying a missing tooth or two. "Anytime, captain."

"Excellent. Angela here will assist you in your repairs."

The smile fell from Buckley's face. "A woman? What is she going to do—knit me a scarf?"

Price sent her a knowing smile and backed up a step. "Not exactly."

Anger boiled beneath her skin. She didn't like her skills being questioned, and she despised feeling useless, but mostly she hated being treated inferior—as a plaything, a weakling to be dismissed. She pointed the hammer straight at Buckley and returned it to her shoulder in demonstration. "I can swing a hammer as well as any man."

Buckley howled with laughter. "All right then, lady. Climb aboard. Show me what's under that skirt."

Price touched her shoulder and whispered into her ear. "Thank you for doing this. Under ordinary circumstances, I wouldn't ask you to."

"I'm just as capable as them."

Price smiled. "In that case, Buckley is a hard worker and a critical asset on our ship, but be careful."

She didn't like that warning. "You aren't coming along?" Angela didn't want him to go. He was the only one she trusted.

"Riley and I will scout around to discover any nearby threats. You're in the hands of pirates who wouldn't cross me, but I do have a few agitators. Keep an eye out for Berger, Liverman, and Vallo." Price walked off after the quartermaster.

Did he say pirates? When Angela had first appeared in the hold, she'd thought the captain was a pirate re-enactor. Fake. For show to sell tickets. But Price had said no one would come to their assistance, because no one would move against the state, and if caught, they'd be swinging at the gallows.

They were pirates.

Buckley stuck his head out the hole and, with several nails between his lips, managed to say, "Lady, are you standing there or helping?" He leveled a rough-cut board into the hole. He struggled to press a nail to the board without it sliding.

To get off this island and find a way home, she had to help. They clearly needed it.

"Hold this here and clear your fingers," Buckley said.

Angela did as directed, and Buckley swung the hammer. He missed the nail several times.

"The captain seems like a nice guy." Angela fished for information. She had nothing better to do but occupy her thoughts.

"Nice? You'd call him 'nice'?" Buckley shrugged. "Such a bland word."

"Why do you say that?"

"I've known that man longer than any others on this ship, except for Lemoine, of course. But he's got himself a lady of his own and left us. Is that what you're planning to do? Steal our captain?"

"I want to go home." Somehow.

Buckley laughed. "Sure thing, lady." From a messy pile behind him, Buckley collected a board, checked its fit, returned it to the stack, and selected a different length. He seemed so...imprecise...to be a carpenter.

"Take your end, hold it snug there, and nail in your side."

"Where did you learn how to do this?"

"Do what?" Buckley hammered in his side, missing every third swing.

"Carpentry."

"Why do you ask?"

Angela's cheeks heated, but with the hole slowly filling, the lighting dimmed. "Just making conversation."

"Hmm. I was a carpenter's mate for years before my master died."

"Oh, I'm sorry. I didn't know."

"Ol' Gerow took a chain shot to the chest, but we captured a fancy prize that day." Angela stared at him, wide-eyed. "Then I stepped up to fill his shoes. Been doing it ever since."

"On the *Sea Lion*? This ship?"

"Of course! Where else would I be from? If I was pressed onto this ship, I would've gone off into those woods to escape once I touched land. No, lady, I'm here because I choose to be, and I won't leave this crew for anything. The sea is the life for me, and hunting is the freedom I need."

Angela cleared her throat, certain she heard wrong. "Excuse me, did you say 'hunting'?"

Buckley cackled. "You stowed away on a ship without checking the crew first? The *Sea Lion* is a vicious predator on the seas, taking what she wants and leaving behind a mess of destruction. Tales stretch from Boston to London and down to Barbados. Just between us, embellished tales only add to our cause. So, whatever you heard may or may not be true, but we never deny the story!"

Angela couldn't picture the captain as a vicious killer, a destroyer of ships and lives. It didn't match what she saw. "Tell me a story—a vicious story."

Buckley bent over the stack of boards and sifted through them. "We found a merchant ship owned by the Sea Trading Company. Overtook her with ease. Those guppies surrendered without a shot fired, which I admit is good for everyone involved. No one wants to careen for repairs when there're prizes to be hunted. Henry was the quartermaster then. We tied up their captain and captured all their remaining cargo. Captain Lemoine himself shot the captain and blew the ship to smithereens. That was more a tale of mercy. The merchant captain didn't suffer his wound for long."

"What about Captain Price? Any viciousness in his past?"

Buckley snorted and spat.

Angela fought a gag.

"If you consider his entire career, plenty. He followed the captain's orders, as we all did, but once he was voted into captaincy, Price has only one thing on his mind."

Curious beyond belief, Angela asked, "What is it?"

"William."

That was not what she expected. "Who's he?"

A shout from above stilled their hammers. The hole was half filled in, but daylight trickled in through many smaller cracks and breaks in the hull, and the stack of boards shrunk by the minute.

"Something's the matter. You best stay here."

In this darkened belly of a pirate ship with spit and who-knew-what-else rotting down here?

No way.

Chapter 10

ANGELA CLIMBED THE HULL, while carrying the hammer, following Buckley against his wishes. She would not be left behind if something happened, and being in the ship's bottom alone gave her the creeps.

Angela straddled the rail. The angled deck was asking her to tumble over and off the other side. With great care, she eased herself down and ducked out of sight. Price had warned her about the agitators, and after her last unpleasant encounter with them, she only wanted to find out if the wreck changed their opinions.

Several men crowded near the mainmast, shouting at each other with nasty scowls. She recognized Berger, Liverman, and Vallo, who, before the wreck, demanded her marooning, whatever that was.

This couldn't be good news.

"What's this about?" Buckley asked the men. "We're trying to work around here."

"The wench stole passage on this ship, but the captain wants her to join our crew like a man. What rubbish is that!" Liverman said.

Men murmured and nodded around him.

Join the crew? Angela only agreed to help fix the damage in exchange for safe passage. No way under any circumstances would she stay here—not with...*pirates.*

"She can hammer a board good as any man," Buckley said. "If you haven't noticed, we're in a bit of a pickle here. We've no time for blabbering."

A warmth of appreciation floated through her. Finally, someone got it.

"She deserves marooning," Berger said, and Liverman nodded smugly. "It's in the articles, *No woman aboard, and any caught are to suffer death.* But we can't maroon her until the ship is fixed. So, I say we pillage nearby towns top to bottom until all the recovered Spanish gold is ours. Spain took the time to recover it. Losing it a second time, at the hands of pirates, no less, shall sting so much worse."

"I'm with Buckley. Marooning her is a waste of breath if the ship's not repaired," McKee, the master gunner said.

"Don't you have more bodies to collect? I think Hayes is still floating down by the hull," Liverman countered. "If we don't abide the rules, we lose ourselves. What's the point of repairing the ship if we ain't a functional company any longer?"

Murmurs of agreement wove through the group.

Liverman continued, "For us to remain together and keep to the cause, I vote for marooning the wench. Row a longboat if we must! Unlike raiding a Spanish territory, Berger, dealing with the woman is both more amusing and less risk."

"I say we allow her to help repair the ship," their third cohort, Vallo said. "It was her cursed luck that caused the *Sea Lion* to kiss the rocks in the first place!"

"But as long as she stays in our presence, the worse our luck shall be!" Liverman countered. "We may as well blow the ship to smithereens then. At least we'd enjoy a show."

If ever there was an appropriate use for the phrase cutting off one's nose to spite their face, Liverman had it down. And since their opinions of her were both depressing and not going to change, Angela crept back toward the rail on silent bare feet.

"Until the captain and quartermaster return, I'm pulling rank here." Buckley said, squaring his shoulders. "That tide is licking our boots. Get back to work."

"Your rank?" Berger said, features darkening. "A scrawny old man? We follow Price and Riley because they can best us in a fight, and they made us promises. But those were broken when the woman was allowed to live. We don't take orders from you." Berger approached the carpenter with a menace on his face that made Angela flinch.

"There she is, the stowaway!" Vallo's finger pointed her out, turning the other angry heads in her direction.

Well, crap.

Buckley turned and frowned at her. The men stalked across the tilted deck like they'd just found their next meal. From Angela's camping experience, she knew the rules of safe wildlife encounters. Most animals were harmless. Squirrels and chipmunks tended to run up trees or down holes and squeak. Deer tended to freeze in fear and bolt away from danger if it approached. Others required more...finesse. In the case of territorial predators, their instincts to chase could be triggered if their prey ran.

Angela stood firm and kept her feet steady, channeling the deer's instincts to avoid a predatory chase.

Whether she'd listened to Buckley's orders to stay in the hull or not, the outcome wouldn't have changed. However, if she'd stayed, she could've run farther before they caught her. No sense dwelling on the past, but her future looked brighter if she had more of it.

"What's marooning?" Angela figured it was nothing good, but delay tactics were all she had.

"We row you out to a desolate spit of land with nary a lick of shade to protect you from exposure. You carry a pistol and shot, and we be generous in allowing three days' provisions," Berger said, encroaching too close.

"Then what?" Angela asked with a lump caught in her throat. She stepped back, on the verge of bolting herself.

"Then we row away." Berger motioned rowing in the air and laughed. Other men around her joined him in their fun.

Angela's mouth fell open. "You can't be serious."

"You broke the rules, you suffer the consequences, wench," Liverman said, closing in on her other side.

"I didn't stowaway!" Angela interrupted, furious at this insane treatment.

"You're off this ship, thief," Vallo said, taking her other side.

Angela stepped back again. A putrid stench reached her nose, reminding her of urine mixed with a mouth that hadn't seen a toothbrush in too many days. And here she thought children were filthy creatures.

"How about I pay for my ride?" Angela lifted the pendant around her neck from the Tall Ships vendor. Although it looked expensive, the amethyst jewel on a copper chain only set her back five bucks. "Take this in exchange for leaving me be."

"Is it valuable?" Vallo asked, eyeing it warily.

"Oh, very." Angela fibbed. "A family heirloom. But I'll give it to you *if* you leave me alone."

"If? Listen lady, if we want to take your valuables, we will, but a deal doesn't change the rules," Berger said.

"Taking valuables is an idea," Liverman said. "Maybe we sell her *and* that necklace instead of maroon her." The men turned to him in disbelief. "Don't go thinking I'm a fickle bastard. Just listen. If we sell her, then we all get a share of her. I know I want a piece."

"I want a share," Vallo said, stalking closer.

"Captain's not here to protect you," Liverman said, and his hungry eyes raked over her body.

Angela dropped the amethyst back against her chest, and she backed up until her butt bumped the rail. She smoothed her tattered skirt and squeezed the handle of the hammer.

Liverman smirked, oblivious to her stance. "She's not Puritan tail, lads, which is a shame, because I'd wager breaking her in would be—" Liverman paused, smirk sliding away.

Angela positioned the hammer over her shoulder, ready to swing. "Touch me, and you'll have a bad day."

Berger laughed in her face and spoke about her like she wasn't there. "She's just a woman. What harm can she do?"

Vallo stopped at her side. All three were within arm's reach, but she couldn't hit all of them at once.

"We have time to decide the desolate spit and fill the longboat with provisions. In the meantime, I'm claiming my share, too," Liverman said with a sinister grin. "We need to vote which man gets the first pump."

"That's enough!" Buckley shouted. "The sea is coming to claim this ship, and she don't care none who's on board. If we can't get her floating in a few hours, we'll be all stranded here another day with Spain lurking in that jungle. I've put up with a lot in my years, but never have my fellow sea dogs been so selfish. You've been hollering about rule breaking and demanding a just punishment, but you have no qualms about breaking your own: fornicating during the account is against the rules, too. Now get back to work, or I'm considering this an official quarrel to settle."

The three agitators turned on Buckley.

"One at a time," Buckley added, steadfast. "Duel to the death. The entire crew as witness."

Berger snarled and sized up the shorter man in a different light.

Buckley tilted his chin up. He was old, worn, and thin, but behind those experienced eyes, he had strength, quickness, and the skills—or at least the courage—to put his money where his mouth was.

"You're going to regret that, old man," Liverman said and pulled on Berger's arm. "Come on fellas. A ship is worthless with a hole in her side."

After darting her a nasty look, Vallo followed the other two. With the men diffused for now, Buckley returned to her side.

"One of these days I'm going to knock the bean off all those dirty dogs. In my days, you respected one another. We all agreed to the rules, but when situations changed, we adjusted. This rigidity they swear by is making them unruly, unfit for the sea." Buckley turned to her. "I don't believe in women on board either, but if one is useful, I take the help. Let's get back to work."

She was thankful someone cared enough to stand up to a group of men for her, and thankful the captain warned her of potential issues. Angela blinked back misty tears.

"Thank you."

"Eh, don't mention it." Buckley waved at the air dismissively.

Chapter 11

As much as Captain Price despised Berger, the man's venomous accusation had been accurate. *And you, captain, steering us straight into Spain's territory like you have a wish for death.* Whether he was brighter than Price believed or the man had questioned Hodgens didn't matter. Price had known the crew wouldn't accept the target he hunted. So, with a little luck from a squall, Price had brought them into Cuba.

Recently, a hurricane had brought down Spain's treasure fleet, and as word spread, pirates, privateers, and Spain herself scrambled to recover what they could.

"What exactly do you expect to find here, Price?" Riley asked as they pushed through the prickly nettles. Daylight would fade soon, but Price had to find it. He needed to know it was here.

"After the Florida wreck, Spain brought their recovered treasure back here, while they coordinated another attempt at a convoy across the Atlantic."

Riley stopped in his tracks. "You want to steal King Philip the fifth's gold right out from under his nose?" Riley approached him and whispered, "Have you lost your mind? Salvaging what we could from the sea is one thing, but sneaking into their territory to take it directly is something else entirely. The men would never agree to that."

Price smirked. "Good thing the squall brought us here."

"Convenient coincidence," Riley said dryly.

"If it's here, a guaranteed prize, they shall change their minds on the risk."

"We shall see," Riley said, and they continued their path through the jungle. Price winced at the prickles on his bare feet, wishing Hayes had worn bigger shoes.

Price needed a large enough prize and a solid win to convince the crew to follow him into a riskier venture, one which offered no compensation. A venture that had plagued Price for months. A venture so ingrained in his psyche, he couldn't quit the account until he'd completed it. Since the day Captain Lemoine resigned and the crew had chosen Price as their new leader, he'd thought of nothing else. The anticipation of seeing the man's shocked and fearful face as Price's cutlass pierced his flesh charged Price, drove his steps. That man deserved worse than a quick slaying, but Price was capable of mercy.

"And what of the woman?" Riley asked.

"What about her?"

"You want to take her along on a prize? See her get cut down by the enemy? Or leave her behind to fend for herself, unprotected?"

The fateful day Price had been given command of the *Sea Lion*, Lemoine had pulled him aside. Price eagerly awaited wisdom from the elder's vast experience on the ocean, but what he'd received softened the excited urges in his veins.

'The gold, silver, and gems make you believe there's this world out there where you can do anything and go anywhere,

but after I met Emily, the real Emily, I learned everything I wanted was right before me. What good is enough silver to buy an estate? What good is enough gold to buy my own island? No jewels in all the world can buy the love, trust, and respect from a woman, and nothing else matters but her.'

'Congratulations, Eric. I wish you well,' Price had told him, a little disappointed.

'Thank you, my dear friend.'

Like Emily, Angela Foxe had magically appeared on the *Sea Lion.* Emily had changed Lemoine's life for the better. Price couldn't say the same for Angela. If she hadn't distracted him, they might not have wrecked at all. But if she *hadn't* been the cause of their wreck, Price would've died. Regardless, that beautiful and strange woman had saved his life. Was some force out there telling him to give up his perilous obligation? To see, as Lemoine had, what was right in front of him?

"She dropped out of the sky and saved my life like an angel." Regardless of her intentions, that was precisely what Angela was—an angel—and Price didn't believe in coincidence.

"She's an angel?" Riley asked with disbelief.

An angel in theory, not reality. Angela was a woman out of time and place, whose perfect arrival saved his life. Price tried to imagine leaving her alone in the camp, hoping locals or Spaniard scouts wouldn't discover her. Hoping she wouldn't go wandering, attempting to find Emily Porter or home by herself. Hoping she wouldn't hate him for making her stay behind, unprotected in this scary world. None of those possibilities, especially the last, could come to pass. "I have every intention of keeping her safe by my side."

"Then why isn't she here now?"

He had a point. "Scouting is dangerous. At this precise moment, she's safest with the crew."

Riley snorted.

"You disagree?" Price's insides swirled. Had he made a mistake? He trusted most of his crew. There were a few he certainly didn't, but he knew the others would keep those few in line.

Ignoring the worrisome thought, Riley asked, "What's that?"

Captain Price pushed aside a frond, revealing a beaten footpath. They were close. The hunt reignited the fire within his veins; excitement stirred afresh. Soon, very soon, that shocked and fearful face was coming.

A twig poked Price in the bare foot, and a shaking of his shoulder brought him from his thoughts.

"What was that? Did you hear it?" Riley asked.

Price was too busy daydreaming of what was to come. "Of what did it sound?"

"Voices and a rustling; men on the move."

Price leaned back on his haunches. Riley bent over his shoulder. Just ahead, two infantry soldiers of the Spanish Armada, wearing clean clothing and carrying muskets with bayonets, causally strolled together. They paced the beaten path for only one reason—they were guarding something, and the boredom on their faces meant they hadn't seen anyone of interest in a long while.

He and Riley retained the element of surprise.

"They aren't here to explore the sugar plantations. Should we take them down?" Riley asked in hushed tones.

"If they continue their course, they shall fall upon our camp and alert others. But if anyone finds their bodies, we shall be actively hunted."

Price trusted most of his men, heartily, to uphold their bond over the account, but if the enemy attacked, did he trust any of them to protect Angela? That was precisely why he wouldn't leave her behind. Suddenly, he wanted to return to camp and never leave her side again.

"So...is that a yea or nay?" Riley asked.

Price slipped a dagger out of its holster. Sometimes survival meant doing things he'd didn't much like. "On my count, we go."

Riley freed a dirk of his own.

As the Spaniard guards approached, Price gestured his countdown. On three, they rushed the men, clamped their hands over their unsuspecting mouths, and jabbed into the men's chests. When the fight drained from the guards, Price finished them off with a deep slice to the throats. Only gurgles and gasps remained. He and Riley dragged the men by their boots deeper into the underbrush and nettles to discourage discovery.

Price pulled a boot off the first man and tried it on. Way too big. He'd trip. Price cast it aside and removed one from the other man.

"What are you doing?" Riley asked.

"How would you like to traverse the jungle barefooted?"

Riley looked at Price's cut and bruised feet. "Do either of them fit?"

Price tossed aside the second boot. "That man has feet of an elephant, and these are too tight."

Riley held out a hand. "Give me the elephant sized boot and you try on mine. Then we'd both have loose boots. Better than you having none, and your vulnerability compromises our mission."

Price handed the quartermaster one of the castaway boots and Riley passed over his own. Price slipped it on, and it fit well enough. "Does it work for you?"

"I must have elephantine feet. I'll wear these." Riley bent and removed the other boot from the soldier.

Price accepted Riley's other and slipped it over his sore foot. He removed the muskets and handed one to his quartermaster while slinging the second over his shoulder. "Much better. Let us keep moving. We're getting close."

Despite being deep into enemy territory, Price continued to feel the pull of returning to Angela's side. Was she safe now? Had other scouts discovered their camp, regardless? The distraction was frustrating. "Riley? Do you have someone back home?"

"Me? No. I had a bride, but it never came to pass."

"What happened?" Price asked.

"Well"—Riley ducked under a swinging branch—"I suppose it depends upon who you ask. My betrothed might say I was the biggest mistake of her life. My father might say I was an imbecile."

Price chuckled.

"But no matter their opinions, her death still haunts me."

"I'm sorry for your loss, mate. I know how hard it is to lose someone you love." Price sighed.

"William?" Riley assumed.

The pain of losing William Price, his older brother, was so great, he'd locked the pain away in the deep fathoms of his heart, fearing its devastating return someday. Not even for Noah Riley would he go diving into those memories. Price had to stay focused on what mattered. "Yea."

The quartermaster must've picked up on his despairing tone, and he changed the subject. "What about you? Any beauty awaiting your arms back home?"

"There's no one for me. Never was." Angela's stunning face and the luck between Emily and Lemoine flashed before him. He swatted it away and kept his feet moving.

A skittering came from nearby. They stopped and listened. The light pattering paused and continued in a direction leading away. Not human. "Likely some critter."

The evening light faded until their eyes struggled to see.

"Why not?" Riley asked, continuing the riveting conversation Price didn't want to have. "You're a strapping captain of virile strength and age, and I'm sure any lady would be thrilled to share your bed."

Price grunted.

Riley waited.

Price sighed again. "When I became of age, I followed my brother into the Royal Navy. My only access to the fairer sex was at port, so I never allowed myself to get attached, and after what happened to William, I didn't have the desire to become attached to anyone again."

"What happened to your brother?"

Riley should know the story. Price needed someone sympathetic to their dangerous mission. "Spain happened."

After a beat, Riley said, "Cryptic as usual."

"You didn't allow me to finish."

"You're too slow, old man," Riley said in jest.

"Old? You're calling me 'old'? Have you no consideration that I'm you ten years in the future?" Price asked, playfully.

Riley beamed. "Precisely. Old."

Price groaned. "*Capitán* Delgado of the *Peibo del ler San Francisco* happened. In short, my brother sacrificed himself so we could escape. Quite genius how he did it, but still, it angers me greatly. So when the *Peibo del ler San Francisco* arrives to convoy the gold, I'll be personally delivering the Spaniards a message."

The quartermaster asked, "You're certain the *Peibo del*-something is headed this way?"

"I made sure of it."

"A convenient coincid—" Riley cut off again with Price's gesture.

A muted murmuring stilled Price's steps. Both men ducked low, and Price brushed aside prickly brambles. A trio of Spaniard guards sat around a table, playing cards by lantern. They spoke to each other. Behind them was a hut made of fronds with no light glowing.

"Do you understand them?" Riley whispered.

"No." Price didn't speak Spanish, and all attempts to learn were met with his steadfast grudge, a bitter pill he couldn't bring himself to choke down.

"How many do you think there are?"

"Appears to be just the three, unless more are sleeping in the hut."

"What are they guarding?"

"Something worth at least five men's lives." With only three left so far, Price liked those odds.

Price rose and, keeping low, gave a wide berth to the hut. A twig snapped and branches rustled behind him.

Price turned and scowled at Riley, but the jungle canopy overhead shrouded his disapproval.

The trio of men paused their game and tilted their heads, listening.

"*¿Es una ardilla, no?*" the first guard asked the other two.

"*Probablemente,*" one man answered with boredom on his tongue.

"*¿Debemos ir a buscar?*" the first guard asked. He sounded nervous. Although Price didn't know what they were saying, he understood they heard Riley's noise and one wanted to investigate. Price leaned lower and waited.

"No. *Juguemos a las cartas. Es más divertido.*" The third guard responded.

Price understood 'no.' When the next player dropped a card on the table, Price crept forward. He waved behind him for Riley to follow. Step by step they circled around to the back of the hut and closed the distance. A small clearing opened the space, leaving their approach easier but also more vulnerable.

"Move quick. Any sound this close will get them moving."

Riley followed, and without disruption, they reached the hut's back wall. The windows were too high to peer inside.

Price knitted his fingers together into a foothold. "Step up."

Riley placed his foot in Price's clasped hands, and Price lifted with all his might—stifling a grunt. His arms shook as he held the man in place long enough for him to see the contents.

Price's hands burned from the strain. "Hurry, Riley."

The quartermaster bent at the knee and dropped himself down. Price brushed off his hands and panted. "What did you see?"

"Chests. Many chests. Only one is open, but it's full of gold coins."

A flutter of excitement tore through Price. "You're certain?"

"Completely."

"Let's return to camp. The crew shall be excited with the news."

As Price led their retreat, relief washed through him. After all these years, the perfect circumstances were within his grasp. All he had to do was lay out the perfect bribe.

Chapter 12

12

Despite her broken family and her mom's cognitive decline, Angela had been a glass-half-full kind of woman, who had plenty to look forward to. And even on bad days, she had no trouble finding the ray of light on a steaming pile of manure. But after the biggest embarrassing public shame of her life, Angela had realized she was forty years old, single, living in an apartment, and working a job she liked but received so much flak for she questioned her own judgment. Her optimism had taken the first bus out of town.

And ever since she'd appeared in this hostile world, she struggled hard to recapture that ray of light. Everywhere she turned was manure. Until now. The sea water had rinsed the putrid stench out of the hull. Angela's lips pulled into a soft smile. Her ray of light was returning...because of poop. And an embarrassingly low bar.

She had to start somewhere, right?

But she worried for Captain Price, who had been gone nearly all day. Was he wandering lost in the jungle? Was he held captive by locals? Was he injured and stuck somewhere? Price was the only barrier between her and the crew's filthy mitts. If they lost him, she lost herself. That wasn't the only reason she didn't want to see him hurt. Angela's judgment had always been crap, clearly, so she questioned it more thoroughly in regards to the captain. They'd shared a moment on the beach, her hand on his chest, and for just a second, she wondered if there could be something between them.

Footsteps creaked behind her. Buckley and Cantu carried the hefty final board down into the hull. With cold, sodden bare feet knee-deep in water, Angela held a candle for them, the only light permitted with Spain lurking about.

Buckley squatted down near the hole, where seawater gushed in, and he shifted the board over his head and into position with Cantu's help. "We had one last replacement board on the orlop deck. If we get this secured, we need to drop anchor. Otherwise she'll be adrift with no crew or supplies when the tide claims her. Hold here."

Cantu kneeled next to the carpenter, and Angela leaned to give them better light.

"If we don't get this blasted piece of—" Buckley trailed off in unintelligible grunts while the men pushed the board against the rushing water. After a day observing Buckley's carpentry skills, hammering nails in the best of circumstances was a challenge.

"Hold it there," Buckley said. "Light closer."

Angela reached the candle out further. The rigging wasn't fully functional yet, but they could escape as it was—assuming they had crew and supplies, of course. The hull had several smaller breaks and leaks in the boards, but Buckley had said the bilge pumps could keep up.

Angela was exhausted, sticky, and tired of being in the sun and eaten alive by bugs. Even when she'd camped with Emily, they'd had a bug-free tent and an air mattress. They'd rested on the beach under shade from massive trees.

There was no rest here.

Not with three men plotting against her. Or Buckley's inaccurate hammering. He swung and missed, spraying water in their faces. The candle flickered and hissed. The carpenter swore as nails dropped into the water. He blindly reached around in the water and made a noise of celebration while lifting two.

"Shall I hammer the board?" Cantu asked.

Buckley made a dismissive noise. "I've been doing this longer than you've been alive. Now, if you do yours, mine shall be easier. Press harder."

Cantu's brows furrowed, but from the shifting biceps in his massive arms, he did exactly that.

Angela's outstretched arm shook with exhaustion.

Buckley's words were punctuated by his hammering. "As I was saying, if we don't get this board into position, we're trapped here another day. It's too dangerous to sit here like ducks. We need to be minimally functional and get the hell out of here." The hammer swung again and again, leaving Angela wishing for painkillers. She tilted her ear against her shoulder and used her free hand to plug her eardrum. Angela closed her eyes and pictured what or where she would be happy...and immediately opened them.

She needed Price to return before they left, or she was going after him.

THE CAMPFIRE CRACKLED IN the woods, disguised by thick vegetation near the cove, and shrouded by supply crates.

Giles turned a crispy pig on the spit, and it smelled like the finest all-you-can-eat buffet. Angela's stomach growled again. The other men broke into various smaller groups to socialize. Buckley stayed near Angela, rustling in the supply crates behind them, because the captain and quartermaster still hadn't returned yet.

The clothing Giles had brought her was certainly less itchy than the shredded polyester costume in a bag, but a shapeless cotton tunic and baggy breeches weren't high up on her list of comfort either. But, she was thankful for non-heeled boots.

"Tie this around you. Should help ya hold them up." Buckley gave her a small length of rope to help cinch her breeches where they belonged. It wasn't awesome, but it would do until she got home.

"Thanks."

"Time to eat. Pass the plates around." Giles held out a serving of steaming meat on a plate, and around the group it passed until the furthest man had his share. Around and around the meat went until finally, Angela had her ration. Ignoring where the plates had last been—in the galley with putrid water running down the decks—and if they'd ever been washed with soap, Angela's empty stomach overrode her brain's hesitation. Juice ran down her fingers and she licked them clean. The men around her softened their stories to murmurs, since they, too, were consumed with feasting.

Angela couldn't help but notice the strong cliques among the crew, not unlike high school—a rite of passage so long ago she'd rather completely forget. Her mother's cheating, and subsequent divorce, were the taboo subject at school.

And she'd thought she'd escaped the gossip of her sleepy small town.

The three agitators, as Price had called them, with their ugly looks over their shoulders and the hushed whispering, only reminded her of those scarred years she'd buried ages ago. She was too tired to confront them, and with the captain still gone, she needed to be careful. These men were only on their best behavior because of Buckley and Cantu's respect for the captain.

What if Price never returned? Angela ate faster. She was not emotionally eating. Nope. She just hadn't eaten a meal in two days, so pigging out was completely normal. No emotional eating here.

After clearing her plate before any of the men, Angela was granted seconds. Giles filled her plate, and Angela thanked him profusely.

Cantu sat on the crate next to her. "Can't say I ever saw a woman eat so much."

"I'm starving. Haven't eaten since yesterday."

"Huh. The captain must find you quite agreeable. I'm not sure I see it myself..."

Angela glared at his gentle insult, and Cantu bit off a hunk of meat and chewed, glancing away as if avoiding the repercussions of that statement. A warmth rushed through her at the thought of the captain liking her, and immediately, she dashed those feelings away.

Price was a pirate, a thief, a scoundrel, someone with lower-than-average morals. And not only that—he led a whole crew of them! The last type of man she'd trust with her heart. After Brandon's public betrayal and her father's complete rejection of her, and numerous less-important boyfriends, Angela was just done with any commitment. And in fact, men altogether.

Cantu swallowed and said, "I only mean I don't see what caused the change of heart."

Despite her unreliable judgment, curiosity got the better of her. "Why do you say that?"

"The last time we had a woman on board, it was Price who insisted on marooning her. So I'm surprised he stood in your defense."

"*Why* did Price want her marooned?"

Cantu spoke with his mouth full. "For stowing away, of course. It's in the rules."

"Then why not me, too? Not that I'm volunteering or anything. I'm just wondering."

"That is the question on everyone's mind." Cantu said.

Did Price want something from her? Did he want to use her for something? A pawn against the agitators? Or was Cantu right—the captain just liked her?

Regardless of her own misplaced feelings, the last one was the hardest to believe. The sooner they fixed the ship, and Price brought her to safety as agreed, she was going home.

Somehow.

At a knock on his door, Marcos would fix her a fabulous martini, and join her and Emily in swapping man-bashing stories. Where was Emily? An empty hole in her heart ached at not knowing where her best friend was.

13

Chapter 13

A RUSTLING IN THE woods nearby quieted down the murmurs of conversations. Branches swayed and cracked. Twigs broke. Everyone turned, facing the sound, and set down their plates. As one, they placed their hands near their weapons. The pork in her stomach sloshed nervously.

Buckley rose from a crate and spoke up. "Arms raised if you want to live."

Buckley and Cantu, like the others, prepared for a fight. Angela set down her plate and wiped her mouth. She had a hammer. As long as the enemy hadn't brought pistols, she had a chance. Angela gripped the handle, oily fingers slipping. She ground her palms against her rough breeches to clean the grease off and find a better grip. With her heart thundering in her ears, Captain Price emerged from the bushes and raised his hands. Riley was just behind him.

"It's us, Buckley. Stand down."

Angela exhaled in relief. She set down the hammer and cleaned her face. Most of the crew smiled and softly cheered his return. The agitators, Berger, Liverman, and Vallo, frowned and turned back to themselves.

Angela's heart fluttered and beat faster, waiting for the captain to seek her out. Price and Riley shook hands with a few of the men and everyone resettled by the fire.

Finally, Price met Angela's gaze. She silently communicated her relief, and she could swear he had been worried for her, too. Angela rubbed her hands on her breeches again and stroked her unruly curls into place. Heat flustered her movements. She pictured herself tackling him and planting a needy kiss on his soft lips. More heat rushed through her. No need for a furnace tonight. Angela wanted to fan her tunic again, but that would make her state obvious.

Holding her fiery gaze, Price said, "Glad to see you in one piece, Angela. Did these old salts treat you well?"

Berger, Liverman, and Vallo cast her an ugly stare, but she wasn't going to let them push her around. She returned a grimace at them. "Most were great."

The three agitators mumbled to themselves, coming to some decision. Berger stood and approached the captain, fury on his furrowed brow. "This is an outrage!" He pointed at her. "She's a hypocrite!"

"How so?" Price asked calmly.

Angela was quite curious herself.

"She pretends to be one of us, keeping quiet on the goings on while you're away, but she stole passage from us. A woman on board is bad luck. She doesn't belong 'ere any longer, and we're overdue in giving 'er just punishment."

"Who else among you believes the same?" Price skimmed the group, but he avoided her gaze.

Vallo and Liverman joined Berger, no surprise there. Giles set down his servingware and stood. Angela's lips parted in horror. The cook treated her kindly! She never guessed his revulsion for her. Giles shifted his weight toward the captain, and Angela exhaled in relief.

"The young lady has done nothing wrong," Giles said. "Having a woman on board is a pleasant change of scenery."

At this visual vote, Cantu and Buckley joined the captain's side. Boatswain Karl Dillon, Hodgens the helmsman, and the master gunner McKee followed on their heels. Angela couldn't help a warmth of appreciation. These men, friends of the captain, not only treated her well, but cared enough to stick their necks out for her. She fought a mist at her eyes.

The rest of the crew, many she hadn't been introduced to, split evenly. A lump formed in her throat. Half the men wanted to harm her.

"Having a woman on board is dangerous for all of us! It divides us. It distracts us. It destroys us," Berger said. With the extra support behind him, his claims became bolder. "She's the cause of the ship sinking—a bad omen, a witch. What'll she do next?"

"What shall it take to make you agreeable, Berger? Liverman, you and Vallo, too?" the captain asked, scratching at his jaw.

"We stick to the rules," Liverman said. "Maroon the wench."

Vallo nodded.

The captain glared at the men supporting Berger. They exchanged wary glances, as if uncertain of their chosen position.

"Well," the captain chuckled. "Unless you see fit to row her to a desolate piece of land yourself, to entertain that idea requires her to join us once again upon the *Sea Lion*."

"Then we leave 'er 'ere," Berger said. "Spain shall dispatch 'er in no time."

Murmurs of agreement came from behind him.

"Is that your final answer, all of you? Leave her here to fend for herself against Spain?"

Vallo looked to the others before nodding. Liverman crossed his arms over his chest, and Berger stepped forward. "She takes provisions for one day, no pistol or shot, and walks. Never to return, and never to step foot on our ship."

Price and Riley exchanged looks, but Angela couldn't guess what was unspoken between them.

How was Angela going to survive on an island full of hostile people? These men spoke English, and they were hard enough to understand. She couldn't imagine Spanish from 1715 was any better. Her small weekend camping trips with Emily meant pop-up tents, groceries, cookware, a vehicle, and several changes of clothes. She wasn't some rugged survivalist, a doomsday prepper with years of supplies. And even if she could capture an animal—and stomached having to kill it—she didn't know how to clean it. And how would she cook it? Angela shivered.

Riley stepped forward. "If both parties cannot come to an agreement, then the rules state the dispute is settled with a dual. Are you both prepared for this?"

The captain stepped toward Berger, shoulders squared and chin up. Her life was literally in Captain Price's hands. She'd rather something else be in his hands, but clearly, not all wishes came true.

"Victor chooses the fate of the woman," the captain said, face drawn in silent fury.

"Victor is breaking the rules," Berger countered. "Then this dual is to the death, not first blood. Winner decides the fate of the woman and earns the captaincy."

"Agreed," Captain Price said.

Angela's mouth popped open. She had never felt more helpless in her life. If Price died, she would be crushed under the worst guilt imaginable. His death would be on her hands, and she could never forgive herself for it. To make this worse—she would be abandoned on this island to die herself, alone. The thought was so terrifying, she couldn't breathe. The only connection she had would be torn from her. As much as she wanted to trust Price's confidence, she had no idea of his capabilities in a fight. Angela leaned over and gripped the hammer. If she was going to be thrown away like yesterday's trash, she was going to fight on her way out. Her hands trembled.

The captain's eyes tracked her movements with the hammer. "Are you worried, my lady?"

Heat rose to her cheeks, both at his confidence and his term of endearment. "I prefer to be prepared. That's all."

Price grinned, easing the butterflies walloping each other in her stomach.

Berger snorted. "When I win, *my lady*," he mocked, "that hammer won't stop me or my men."

Vallo and Liverman snickered.

"Then all parties are in agreement with the terms," Riley said and sent a dark look at the captain before backing to a safe distance.

None of the crew on the captain's side spoke up. That wasn't reassuring.

The captain drew a sword and Berger copied, while the rest of the crew backed away, leaving ample space to avoid collateral damage. The fire crackled, and golden light flickered across the angry men's faces. Only one would survive the fight.

"On my count, begin." Riley counted down from three, and the swords crashed together with a sharp clang. Both cutlasses withdrew and crashed again and again. Angela flinched with each strike. Firelight glinted against the sharp blades. The captain dodged a swipe from Berger, stepped forward, and swung. His opponent leaped back, but a slice ripped open Berger's shirt. The swords locked, and the men's faces pulled close, straining in hate and fury.

Berger flung himself back and dodged the captain's strike again. The agitator rolled forward, kicking up sand. With an arc of his blade, he struck the captain, who tumbled backward to the ground, fist pressed to his chest.

Angela gasped and hugged the hammer. It wasn't over. It couldn't be over just like that.

The crew shouted at each other. The anger from both sides brought tears to her eyes. This was all her fault. The captain's impending death, the destruction of the crew, the destroyed ship and all the lives lost. If she hadn't come here, they would still be sailing the seas as one—focused, committed, and not distracted by her.

Angela wanted to run away, to save them from this horror, and to save herself the deep guilt of having caused it all. But the captain was on the ground, and Berger accepted congratulations from his side of the crew.

They considered it over. Angela squeezed the hammer. She should use the upper hand to her advantage and take out Berger. Maybe she'd earn enough respect to be left alone—to die in peace somewhere lost on this island. But she couldn't leave the man who'd saved her and treated her with utmost respect. She swiped away the tears blurring her vision. Wanting desperately to rush to his side, but not risking a deviation in Berger's attention.

Berger holstered his blade to pats on the back. One by one, Berger's half of the crew approached her with snarls of hate. Angela squeezed the hammer. In the storm, she knew she couldn't take on three men with her hammer. Now she certainly couldn't take on a dozen. Angela met Buckley and Cantu's eyes, silently pleading for help.

They gazed at the fire.

Price's half didn't come to stop them. The dual was final, and the terms were set in stone. She was to be left behind, but the looks on their faces meant they wouldn't leave her in peace.

The captain shifted on the ground. Angela only spared him a glance, so the others wouldn't be tipped off. And no one else paid him attention. It wasn't over.

"As much as your presence tore this crew apart," Berger said, now pulling ahead of his men as if he deserved dibs, "I have to thank you. I'm the captain now, and I'll take my congratulations the proper way."

The men behind him chuckled in a way that churned her gut.

Liverman shouted, "On your knees, wench!"

Another said, "I only want her mouth. You dirty dogs can have her other holes."

The chuckles returned.

"Buckley? Cantu?" she found her voice—softer and less commanding than she was used to.

"Rules are rules," Buckley said with the shrug, failing to look her in the eye. "Sorry, ma'am."

Riley said, "Captain's orders are followed. Berger won the duel, so his rule goes."

Angela couldn't believe they'd be this barbaric. Where was their humanity, and how the hell did Emily admire these bastards? "You can't be serious! I didn't do anything to you, and I certainly didn't ask for this." Angela swatted the filthy paws reaching out to her.

"It's what we all signed," Cantu added, turning away like he was unable to watch what happened next.

"Let it be known! As captain, I'm making changes. Our last rule, *no boy or woman to be allowed amongst them. If any man were found seducing any of the latter sex, and carried her to sea, disguised, she was to suffer death. While seducing* is still forbidden..." Berger trailed off to build suspense. The men paused, a little confused while waiting for the announcement. "All the sex you want is acceptable by all hands at any time unless in battle."

The men chuckled and hollered their appreciation, and when their short celebration was over, they approached like wolves to their prey. Playing deer would no longer work.

"Leave me alone!" Angela pleaded softly.

They didn't.

Chapter 14

PRICE'S VISION RETURNED, FUZZY at first, and then clearer. Where was he? What happened? Searing heat stung across arms and sides. Warm liquid drizzled down his skin.

The fight.

Price moved his sword arm, still gripping his weapon firmly. The cuts were not fatal, but if he didn't breathe soon, it would matter naught. His lungs felt deflated, like a hefty weight pressed against his chest, and no matter his struggle to inhale, they would not cooperate.

His head pounded, and a spot on the back of his skull raged in pain. Price flinched and shifted, landing his wounded head on the soft sand. Minor relief.

The air wouldn't come.

His lungs felt afire. This was the end. He'd been bested by an opponent sure of foot and quick of eye, a fierce competitor. Price did not expect this outcome. He'd failed avenging his brother. He'd failed his crew. But most of all, he'd failed Angela. His promise to her was broken. What was the value of a man without trust in his word?

Half his sworn crew, bound by the articles, suddenly threw away all they'd agreed to, surrendering to their libidos. They intended to defile the woman in a way that made his blood curdle.

He'd gone from boy following his brother, to a man thrusting headfirst into the life he'd dreamed of, to a man broken by loss. Of all the things he could've imagined accomplishing, the one regret plaguing him at this moment was his failure to find a woman who loved him. He'd never know the loyalty, trust, and respect of a woman warm in his bed. Someone to share his dreams and fears, who wanted to be with him. Someone he could devote his life to. Someone like...Angela.

The revelation surprised him.

Anger at his failure, at Berger's threats on the other side of the campfire, and the cackles of the animals around her, lit a fire within. His lungs inflated with a deep gasp of air.

It wasn't too late for him to take back control, realign the crew, and rescue the woman he found himself dreaming of.

Even if he couldn't keep her.

From the tips of the toes to the hairs on his head, an energy surged through him like a hurricane's swell.

Angela needed saving. Angela needed him.

Price climbed to his feet and rubbed the back of his aching head while stalking closer to his usurper.

BERGER PUSHED HER CLOSER to the fire. Heat scorched her skin. The other men untied their breeches, cackling like drunken frat guys and arguing over their position in line. Angela didn't know how to avoid the inevitable.

The captain's sword shifted in the air, and Price slowly climbed to his feet. He rubbed the back of his head and checked his bleeding chest wound. The crew was too busy with her to notice, and she declined to alert them. His presence was the only thing keeping her level-headed—she wasn't alone against all these animals.

Berger approached her, scowling, and he squeezed her arm.

"Let me go!" she shouted, twisting out of Berger's grip.

Another man locked on her arm in an instant, freezing her in place. A third man squeezed the nape of her neck.

Price moved closer, cracking his neck, sword positioned to strike.

Angela squeezed her hammer and swung at the man holding her arm. He took a bruising thump to the thigh and released her. Others backed up, except for the one clamped on her neck.

"Get off of me!" Angela swung the hammer behind her.

The cackling captor caught her wrist and squeezed. "On your knees, where you belong."

Angela dropped the hammer, yelping in pain.

Price stood behind Berger and leveled the sword at the back of the man's neck. "Next time you believe you're the victor, check your opponent, for it could cost your life."

The color drained from Berger's face. His lips parted, and his eyes widened. Lifting his hands in surrender, he turned to face the captain.

The half of the crew in support of Price smirked but didn't move to assist. Jerks. The other half released their predatory postures, and the man clamping on her neck released her.

"Be that as it may, the duel is not over." Berger parried the blade away from his throat and performed a duck and roll maneuver. Leaping back to his feet, he unsheathed his sword in challenge. "So let us finish this. I have more important business now."

With eyes on Berger, Angela discreetly collected her hammer with a firm grip. The captor behind her noticed her movement and fastened his hand on the nape of her neck again. Gritting her teeth, Angela swung hard at the man, impacting his abdomen. With a grunt, the captor folded and fell to his knees.

Another man grabbed her arm. "Try that again and you won't see daylight before each of us has a turn with you." He moved to take the weapon from her, but Angela swung it at his hand and quickly adjusted to swing at his head. The creep ducked, and Angela kicked him in the crotch.

The man folded and fell to the sand. Anger flashed across his beat red face, and Berger's other supporters surrounded her, ready to take their turn in subduing her, as if she'd challenged their manhood.

The captain and Berger circled and struck, blades swooping and crashing through the air. The captain couldn't help her now. But knowing he was on his feet empowered her. She wouldn't give up.

Angela lifted the hammer over her shoulder. Her stomach swirled with nerves, and her hands shook with the adrenaline, but pretending to be strong was a better choice than showing her fear. She had nothing else to lose. "Who's next?"

Three of the agitators cackled. Liverman said, "Did you hear that, fellas? The wench wants a fight!"

Price's supporters whispered to themselves, a quiet argument with hands moving.

"I'll take a fight with her. Sounds like a good time to me." A filthy miscreant grinned, missing half his teeth, giving her the impression the man didn't usually win those fights. Not that she was willing to place bets right now.

Quartermaster Riley led the group of Price's supporters, and they surrounded the agitators. "All of you, keep your hands off the woman or lose your fingers."

Several of the men turned to the threat with scowls twisting their features. Cantu towered over Liverman, and the instigator leaned around the bigger man to see the status between Berger and the captain. Both men suffered bleeding cuts and torn clothing. Both panted heavily, exhaustion haunting them. No matter the outcome, the fight was certain to end soon.

The crew opposing the captain shared glances and shrugs, an internal war waging over whether to comply or rebuff.

"We were a crew once," Cantu added. "A trustworthy crew bound by a single goal: claiming freedom for ourselves. And now we're split even, fighting each other, when never has there been a time when we need to stay together more. How can we trust you aboard the *Sea Lion*? But neither can we sail without you. Drop this crusade you're on now or we will find a new crew."

Liverman chuckled nervously. "You don't scare us."

"I'm only trying to delay you."

Liverman cocked his head in confusion.

A gargling groan came from behind them, followed by a thud. The statuesque Cantu smiled, and the divided crew turned to see the outcome. Angela's heart caught in her throat. She pushed through the men, still gripping the hammer, and stopped short.

Captain Price kneeled on the sand, head hung low, blood smeared all over him. Berger's body rested in the sand at the awkward angle he fell. The captain wiped his face with his forearm and climbed to his feet.

Price wiped his sword on Berger's body and sheathed it. Casually, he strolled around the fire and faced Angela. Heat rushed through her body as he stood only a foot from her. She wanted to embrace him, treat his wounds, care for him. Seeing him in pain hurt her. Tears pricked her eyes. Not only had he survived, but he'd suffered on her account, and now she would be saved a fate worse than death.

The captain cleared his throat.

Standing so close to her, Price's heart thundered in his ears, but he regretted not a second of his decision to challenge Berger. Had he known he'd win? Berger had far more agility and immature confidence, but Price had cunning and patience. In essence, no, Price wasn't certain he'd win, but he had been certain he couldn't leave Angela in danger, and that had been the only solution.

"All those who dissented from my leadership, leave immediately," Price said, addressing half the crew while gazing into Angela's beautiful brown eyes. She was afraid, but there was relief and perhaps a dash of lush in there.

Desire and need flooded his veins, but he couldn't kiss her. Not like this. Not in front of the crew. He'd lose his authority in a flash—no matter what his triumph proved.

The men glanced at each other, as if unwilling to think for themselves, and no one moved.

Price gritted his teeth. Half this crew betrayed his leadership, and now that they'd lost, these men were too cowardly to uphold their position of dissent. "You'll be allowed safe exit from the area, and no one will hunt you down. Go. If you don't want to be on my crew, I don't want you either."

Buckley and Cantu stared down Liverman and Vallo, but still no one moved or spoke.

Price addressed his most frustrating men. "Liverman, Vallo? Anything to say on your own behalf?"

"If it pleases the captain, I shall stay on the crew," Liverman said, toeing the sand and keeping his eyes down.

It certainly didn't, but Price needed men to sail the ship, and there were no guarantees he would find suitable replacements on this island. "Agreed. Vallo?"

"I'll remain as well," Vallo said, as Price expected. The quiet man may have been one of the agitators in the crew, but that was his job, and Price was convinced of his loyalty.

"Anyone else want to speak up? We are all listening."

The murmurs began and when they cleared, all hands agreed to stay—both a relief and a stress. Now he'd have to watch his back until he replaced half the crew.

"Let me make this clear: if any of you attempt to harm Angela again, you'll all be marooned, even if I must sail this ship on a skeleton crew! Now, get some sleep."

The crew dispersed, but Angela remained next to him. He offered his hand. "Come with me."

Liverman scowled, but if the man had anything to say, his chance was over.

After a second's hesitation and a quick glance over her shoulder, she accepted. The captain took her soft hand and led her away from the crew, deeper into the woods, into the darkness.

Price needed privacy.

Leading her through the easiest, clearest path, he held branches out of her face and pointed out obstructions to step over. Behind a thick tree, he turned around.

"What is it? What's wrong?" Angela asked. "Are you seriously hurt? Are you going to be okay?"

Bluish light pierced the canopy overhead, shining an eerie but beautiful glisten on her features. He couldn't get the woman out of his mind: where she came from, where she planned to go. How was she going to reach her destination safely? Price didn't want to leave her side.

"I tried to keep an eye on you, but Berger's quick feet and an unfortunate stone in the sand distracted me. Did the crew harm you?" Price brushed a lock of long hair over her shoulder.

Angela touched his hand, not to stop him, but to hold him. "You almost died, and you're worried about me?"

Price remained silent, answering the question for her.

"Oh." Angela rubbed an arm. "They didn't. They tried, but no, they didn't hurt me. I think I might've hurt a few of them." She lifted the hammer. "This is my new friend."

"Keep it."

"These men don't seem to like you very much."

"We are business associates. As long as we agree on the goal, we are in accord, but if not, well, you've seen what can happen."

"Killing each other is a little extreme, isn't it?"

"Depends. In these trees lies outposts for the Spanish Crown, enemies of England. If they find us, or you, they shall have no qualms about killing us. They see us as less than men, as animals. They'll do much worse to you first, which is why I shall do anything it takes to keep you safe."

Angela shifted her weight and glanced off to her side before locking eyes with him again. Heat bloomed in his chest like the petals of a Mexican daisy opening for his sun.

"Why me? Why are you risking your life to help me?"

Price couldn't put to words exactly why he was so drawn to her, so he gave her a reasonable reply. "I promised you safe passage."

"Oh." The disappointment on her intelligent face caused the fire to roar through his body. She wanted more than safe passage. As did he.

"Kiss me," he whispered, hoping beyond everything she didn't reject him, hoping that he hadn't misread, hoping...for a possibility.

Angela moved her hands to his neck, thumbs stroking his jaw. His heart pounded in his chest. He heard nothing but the swish of his own blood and nearby critters. Angela leaned forward, pressing against his injured chest, but he swallowed back the gasp. This was too important. He needed this.

He needed her.

Angela's soft lips gently pressed his, and every worry and concern melted away. His arms wrapped around her, holding her tight, never wanting to let go. He shifted positions, tasting her, teasing her, losing himself entirely. She was more than he'd ever expected or hoped for.

He understood why Lemoine risked everything for Emily, because Price would do anything for Angela.

Slowly, she pulled back and studied his face as if questioning her actions. She smiled, wrinkling the corners of her eyes. That wasn't enough. He needed more.

Price buried his fingers into her tangled hair, ignoring the pokes of the bobby pins, and found her lips once again. He pressed harder, working her sweet lips, driving his desire wild. Their breath fought through their noses, and Angela panted, pressing herself against him and pushing them both against the tree.

He wanted all of her.

But that would make him no different from the other men, and if they were caught, he'd be back in the same position as before: challenged for the captaincy and Angela's life. Only this time, all the dissenters, and perhaps many of his supporters, would simply execute him. Reluctantly, Price slowed and released her.

Angela beamed under the moonlight, and she rubbed her arm. "Wow."

He had no idea what that breathy word meant. To think he failed to please her was worse than a sword to the chest. "Is that good?"

"Very."

Price's lips pulled wide, and she raked his unruly hair out of his face, tucking it behind his ears.

"I like your earring. I wonder if you have others elsewhere?" Angela asked with a teasing lilt.

"Someday you'll have to look for yourself."

She chuckled. "Thank you, by the way, for saving me from those men."

"You've already thanked me plenty."

Angela laughed, but a twig snapped behind them, silencing her. Price leaned around the tree, and a rustle of footsteps darted off into the filtered light.

"What was that?" she asked.

"Not a what, but a whom." Price squinted into the light to identify the man, but he wouldn't chase that fool's errand, leaving Angela alone. "I realize you aren't a sailor of the *Sea Lion*. You didn't read and agree to the rules, as I have. If any consequences become of this, I need you to know two things."

Angela waited patiently.

"The crew and its rules are my responsibility, and I shall take all the blame. And two, whatever the consequence, it was worth it."

"What are you talking about?"

"Women on board are forbidden, hence their insistence on a stiff punishment for stowing away, as are any relations between women and the crew."

"The rule Berger wanted to change."

"Right."

"I didn't hurt anyone. We didn't hurt anybody. Why does my presence matter at all?"

"Women are a distraction. The rule is to keep the crew agreeable and rational. Focused."

Angela frowned. "What about the gay men?"

Price didn't know what that had to do with anything. "Sometimes they are," he said slowly. "No one minds, as long as their activities don't interfere with the men's sleep."

"That's hardly fair, giving a pass to men but not women." She sighed. "If that witness says anything, what are they going to do this time?"

Price gently touched the woman's jaw. Judging by the direction of the mysterious man's retreat, he wasn't *Sea Lion* crew at all. "Come with me. We're going to find a new place to rest for the night."

Angela took his hand. He'd keep both eyes open the rest of the night if he had to.

Chapter 15

ANGELA OPENED HER BLEARY eyes to check the time, but there was no alarm clock. No end table. No Serta. Her aching back and neck reminded her an air mattress was a necessary minimum when sleeping away from her supportive bed, but the aches quickly receded when she found who was next to her—the captain, sprawled on his back on a prickly bed of flattened plants. His head rested in his hands, elbows out, eyes closed. Hating these inches between them, she wanted to get closer. She wanted to cuddle up on his chest. Her excuse for not making a move? The gash in his skin. Angela didn't want to hurt him.

Angela closed her eyes against the brilliant oranges and purples of sunrise, remembering the kiss that swept her clear into a dream. An energy pulsed through her like an invisible force—just her and the captain together in their own private bubble of safety.

Nothing else would ever compare.

But even back home, she could never stay in bed all day, and coffee called. Angela rose and stretched the aches. As the morning sun penetrated through his off-white tunic, revealing his shape underneath, she gazed at his delicious form but frowned at the mar to his flesh. She leaned down to shake a shoulder and wake him, but his hand caught hers before she touched him.

"I'm already awake." Captain Price popped his eyes open, meeting her gaze.

Heat flushed her cheeks at being caught. He brought her hand to his mouth, and he kissed her knuckles. A deep flutter erased her need for coffee. She was wide awake now, and she noticed the dark rings under his eyes.

"Did you get any sleep?"

"I shall catch sleep when it's safe to do so."

Guilt nagged at her. He'd suffered on her account...again. One thing she learned since landing here in time: some pirates were true gentlemen. And now she wanted to know his story. How did he end up with these barbarians, and why hadn't he left?

The captain grunted sitting up. Angela held out a hand to help him to his feet. Captain Price stared at it, confused.

"Take my hand," she insisted.

"I don't understand why."

Angela snorted and grabbed his hand. She pulled him, and he stood with the assistance. "That's why."

"Where you're from must be a strange place." His hand pressed against his wound. "But, thank you."

He'd never believe her even if she tried to explain, so she had no intention of trying. "Do you need something for that?" She pointed at the blood-soaked material.

"It's more pride than injury. Let us return to camp. Giles should have breakfast shortly, and I need to return to repairing the ship. Do you still have your hammer?"

Angela bent down and lifted it. "It's right here."

"After the loss of Berger and the aggressions against you, I hope you'll continue to assist us. We need you."

There was something deeper to those words, something far beyond patching a hole in the hull. Angela didn't want to pry, so she said the first thing that came to mind—getting off this dangerous island. "I don't want to be stuck here any longer than you do."

"Excellent. I have a speech to give the crew while they break their fasts."

What could that possibly be? Angela was curious but not enough to prod. Hopefully, they would get off this island and then she had to figure out how to get home, but landing in US soil was a good start. A pang of sadness rolled through her.

THE CREW GATHERED AROUND the fire as Giles dished out portions of the morning's pig. Although everyone passed the plates without a fuss, and ate quietly, the angry stares shivered her spine. Liverman and Vallo were still upset with her presence, and too many for comfort sat by them. It hurt. Those men meant nothing to her, but the hatred they displayed honestly hurt.

When she'd met Brandon Spindleton, and finally believed he was genuinely interested in her, Angela assumed his upbringing meant he'd be a perfect gentleman. From a childhood of rejection and poverty, she'd truly thought she'd caught her break, a real life Cinderella. But after months of replaying every memory, she believed Mrs.

Spindleton wanted her son's hidden life under control to prevent a scandal, and she'd chosen Angela to control her, strip her of her rights, and bury her under legal documents. Despite the legacy needing protection, Angela couldn't figure out why she wasn't enough to rein in Brandon's wild ways. He had to be ashamed of her or he simply never cared at all. Thankfully, Angela got out of there before it was too late.

All she really wanted was to be accepted and loved. So why, with her newfound self-esteem did the pirate crew's rejection bother her so much?

Captain Price respected her, treated her like an equal—which was baffling in these times. He fought for her and saved her life. The man even stayed awake all night just to keep her safe. His lips were amazing, but beyond that lustful exterior, he dispatched one of his own for her.

Angela's eyes drifted to the captain, who ate with the rest of the crew, keeping an eye on her. Captain Price put her first. He wasn't ashamed of her—if he could understand what her job entailed, anyway—and he did care. If Angela allowed herself to open up to him fully, to fill that broken hole in her heart, with him from the past and her from the future, how would it work?

Captain Price set down his plate and brushed his hands clean. "We all know we're currently stranded on Cuba, surrounded by Spain, but I have a plan."

The *Sea Lion* crew closed in tight, elbow to elbow, and grease shined on their dirt-streaked faces. Sand snarled the hair on their heads and faces. Despite their repulsive self-care, their eyes were sharp.

"There's a settlement to the west and forts to the east. No warships are presently at anchor. The first priority is repairing the *Sea Lion*. To prepare for departure, a small group will join Giles in procuring provisions and additional fresh water. The locals offer everything we need to set sail, but we risk their betrayal to the Spaniards. At my authorization, Giles shall take a bribe with him. Giles, pick two men."

The cook named a pair who smiled and stood eager for their assignment. Captain Price handed the cook a pinch of gold coins and pointed for them to move out at once.

"With the expectation all hands maintain the repair schedule throughout the day, at nightfall, we shall break into two groups ready for action. Riley will lead one with Karl, in charge of heaving to immediately upon our return." The captain listed off the names he expected to follow the quartermaster. McKee and Hodgens were also chosen for ship duty. "The second group will join me. Last night, Riley and I discovered treasure recovered from the Spanish wreck hiding in a hut, guarded by a handful of men. We must raid the hut before the warship arrives to collect and transport it home."

"Wait," Angela said, confused. The men faced her, half of them fill with utter disgust. Swallowing back their glares, she said, "A warship...so, a ship full of healthy, well-rested, and fully armed men are coming to collect an extremely valuable state-own treasure. I have a hammer. Many of you have swords and a few have pistols. No offense, seriously, but what are you going to do against a small army?"

Angela hadn't met true undiluted scorn until now. If looks could kill...

"Of course the wench wouldn't understand..." Liverman cut in.

Captain Price smiled gently. "That's why we move quickly, quietly, and under the cover of darkness. An army would be impossible, but we can take on a handful."

Angela had no reply to that, and the murmurs from the promise of an easy hunt returned.

"Treasure without having to take a prize for it?" one man asked with growing excitement.

"Treasure without having to dive for it?" another asked, equally happy, since most men on ships apparently didn't know how to swim.

Price nodded at the growing excitement. "All the costs from the squall damage and lost life shall be covered in full with more money leftover than any one man could reasonably spend."

"We can live like kings? Take no orders? Hide from the Crown's noose forever?" the first man asked. Several others shared looks of bursting excitement.

Captain Price smiled hungrily. "Precisely."

The men exchanged laughs and beaming grins.

Angela couldn't help but be appalled at their greed, but their lives were different from what she was used to. Brandon Spindleton's estate wasn't altruistic, but as far as she was aware, the Spindletons weren't engaged in active piracy either.

Captain Price paused from his celebratory speech to glance her way, and at the look of disappointment, his smile faltered. While the men eagerly organized their assignments and plans, the captain approached her.

She stood to meet him. "You didn't say what my assignment is." As if she was important enough to consider. As if she was one of them...

"Come with me." Price took her by the hand, leading her away from the group planning.

"What a minute there!" Liverman shouted and stood.

The captain stopped, sighed, and turned around, but he declined to address the man. Captain Price only stared with hatred and warning.

"You won the duel, so you decide the woman's fate, but that doesn't give her rights to be on the ship, and it certainly doesn't allow the captain to have sex with her," Liverman said, gaining the attention of the rest of the crew. "If you get a turn, then we all get a turn, such is the way on this ship!"

Men murmured, and a couple let out shouts of agreement.

The captain addressed Liverman while still grasping her hand. "There is no sex aboard the *Sea Lion*, or among the crew while still on the account. I did sign the rules, as did you, and unlike you, I have never broken them. I am afraid, Liverman, the squall has knocked and tossed the wits from your head. But fear not! The lady and I shall go seek them out. Come, my lady."

Cantu and Riley snorted and covered their laughs. Buckley barked out unrestrained laughter while others simply smiled. Liverman frowned, blushed bright, and sat down.

Angela covered her own smile.

The captain pulled her through the dense Cuban jungle until far from earshot. Angela's heart raced in her ears, hoping for a chance to steal another kiss.

He stopped near a thick fern. "Now that Liverman and his mouth are out of our way, I've weighed both options thoroughly, and it's a risk either way, but I want you to accompany me on the raid."

Her? Captain Price wanted her to hunt down some treasure with him? How was this plan in any way ensuring her safety? Perhaps she misunderstood. "Ummm. What?"

"I split the crew to ensure the best possible outcome based on trust. Riley is my right-hand man, and I'm giving Riley the thorns in my side. I can't take them with me, because I don't trust them to not betray me to Spain. That means you must join me. With you by my side, I can protect you, but if you insist on staying with the ship, I cannot presume Riley's team shall restrain themselves, given the *enormous* temptation to give in to their baser desires." Captain Price pointedly raked her body with his hot eyes.

Heat rose in her cheeks, but something he said stood out. "You don't think much of your crew, do you?"

"Men with a goal in common can be a powerful force, but when those goals are disrupted, the men split, and nothing remains predictable. Trust is destroyed, chaos ensues, and the entire mission falls apart. I won the duel. It's my choice to leave you stranded on this island or take you with us. I should think my preference is clear. And since I cannot return you home safely at this moment, I need you to stay by my side."

Remembering what the captain said about a warship full of trained soldiers, Angela swallowed a thick lump in her throat. Fighting off a dozen filthy pigs with a hammer sounded easier. Instead, a dozen men headed into a fight against a possible hundred. Those odds were so much worse.

"I know what I am asking of you," Captain Price said, holding her arms in desperation. "But I believe you can do this. I will keep you safe. I promise you."

A flush of heat warmed her chest, a lightness, a foreign sensation of being important. She was *numero uno* to someone else, and she wanted nothing more than to stay by the captain's side. He was the only one she fully trusted.

"I'll go with you."

Price pulled her against him, and his lips found hers in a stolen secret moment, but it was over so fast, she wasn't sure it happened.

That would be a daydream to hold on to.

Chapter 16

THE MEN WORKED AS a tireless team all day. Karl's crew replaced the rigging with spares from below deck, but the extra set was a tangled mess, and shouts of frustration liberally flowed from him and the men assisting. That was not a job Price would ever care to do.

Cantu cut down and chopped up a tree for replacement planks, and even with an assistant sawing, producing viable boards would take a long time. Price had to urge Cantu to use the boards as they were, but the perfectionist fought, grumbling under his breath. Time was of the essence.

Buckley kept his group in line patching and tarring the smaller wounds in her side, and Price leaned back on a freshly filled barrel of water, giving his aching neck and spine a break. He mopped the sweat from his forehead and checked on the wound in his chest. He needed fresh bandages, but there were none left.

Watching the men work as a coordinated team, too busy for drama, brought a smile of nostalgia to his lips. Just like the good old days when men focused and cared about nothing but getting the job done. Mountains could be moved with enough hands willing. And that wasn't the best part. Last night, calms waters brought in a gentle tide and the *Sea Lion* lifted up. Their laborious efforts would succeed, and when the tide returned tonight, regardless of weather conditions, the anchor shall keep her in place until the time they needed to escape.

Everything was moving along according to plan.

Except one thing.

Angela tirelessly hammered in new boards all around the hull. Her laboring alongside his men pained him deeply, but she'd insisted. What world could a woman come from where work such as this was expected of them? Certainly no high society. In any case, Price had no choice but to accept her assistance. All able-bodied men were forbidden from idleness unless taking a needed break.

Including Price. With a final deep exhale, Price lifted off and headed back into the shade. He'd been assisting master gunner McKee with salvaging weapons from the hull for maintenance and repair for tonight. Typically, it wasn't a captain's job, but he was leading the raid on the treasure hut, and he wanted a firsthand count of their serviceable weapons. Price lowered himself across from McKee at a makeshift table—an empty barrel, too damaged to hold liquids.

McKee unscrewed and removed the lock assembly of a pistol, checking for saltwater corrosion, and inserted a plug in the vent hole. Price lifted the next pistol in line, inspected its condition, and filled and emptied the barrel to wash out the black-powder fouling.

"Having a skirt on board is bad luck," McKee said over the soft noises of metal clashing and clattering as they worked.

"You, too?" Price sighed. "I need men who can focus on the account, not on a woman."

The crew's backlash was not unexpected, but its continued presence was a meddlesome pest. Not one man on the crew could see reason above breasts. Although, if the situation were less dire, Price would gladly admire Angela's ample soft chest for hours on end. A leisure he hadn't sought in ages.

"We're on land. A woman can make use of herself easily. Why not send her away and remove the wedge in the crew?" McKee asked calmly, keeping his eyes on his cleaning.

"We lost too many good men in that squall. Navigating these waters is difficult enough with all hands."

"She can sail?" McKee lifted a brow.

"No, but she's helpful." Regardless of her capabilities, Price had promised himself he wouldn't allow another's noble efforts to cause their death. Not for him. Not again.

McKee uttered a noise of amusement. "I fear this is history repeating itself. Do you not fear Lemoine's end?"

Price's hands stilled in their cleaning. Captain Eric Lemoine, retired, resided in a seaside plantation with a woman, someone he tended to and someone who held him accountable. That was an enormous responsibility. After all his years of freedom, would Price want such a thing? His gaze traveled to the hull, where Angela hammered away on a patch. A glimmer of hope fluttered through his mind.

Price tried to picture it, but he couldn't reconcile their two worlds. Angela only wanted to go home—back to her family. Who was he to stand in her way? The stolen kiss had been unbecoming of a man, but he couldn't help himself at the time. Price already had his future carved out. After his business on this island was complete, he was retiring with his bountiful share on the mainland, where his feet could plant firmly on the ground. Where food was a short stroll away. Where the sea was quiet, the air was dry. Only after he found a man who'd guess an oar to be a strange shovel, then that was where he'd find his peace. If he survived at all.

"Lemoine's end shall not be mine."

"Of course not. You'll get yourself killed long before then," McKee said.

Price shot him a sharp look.

McKee poured black powder down the barrel. "Your crusade against Spain is not the secret you think it is, not for us who've been around. Frankly, so long as my pockets are heavy, I care not who we fight." He paused, and Price returned his attention to his pistol.

"But life at sea is too short as it is, so if you feel your heart is screaming at you, listen to it. Don't waste a chance at happiness."

Price wouldn't waste it, he just couldn't see it.

"And if your gaying instrument is shouting in your ears, do us a favor and go box the Jesuit. Last thing Liverman and Vallo need is more fuel for their fire, and they'd be right. It's the rules, captain."

Taking advice from a younger man never settled well in Price's gut, but he couldn't deny the misplaced wisdom. "You need not concern yourself with my affairs. I retain control over my own body, unless angered enough, then I cannot say for sure what my trigger finger shall do."

McKee rammed the rod down the barrel harder than necessary, but without a reply, Price presumed his point was received. Unlike some of the baser animalistic crew, Price was a gentleman, capable of maintaining himself.

After cleaning the next pistol, he passed it to McKee for loading. There weren't enough pistols for each of the raiding crew, but if Price succeeded in his plan, no one would fire a single shot. Plans rarely went according to plan.

McKee placed a shot over the patch and pushed it into place carefully. "That's the last one."

"Get them dispensed to the men accompanying me tonight. Check on Peter Gunner. Make sure the guns are in working order and the munitions are ready. When you see us returning, likely at a swift pace, alert Riley to weigh anchor and get us underway immediately. I want you to have men at the guns prepared to return fire."

"And if the *Sea Lion*'s sails are not ready?"

"Make them ready." There was no alternative option. They must succeed or die trying.

"Can do, captain. Wish I was going with you."

Captain Price stood and sheathed a pistol for himself. "I'd prefer you at my side, but I need you here."

McKee smiled. "Get out of here and make history."

Price planned on it.

Chapter 17

EVEN OUT OF THE sunlight, Angela's itchy tunic clung to her sticky chest. She swiped her forehead, now understanding why the pirates wore bandannas. With the stifling air in the lower decks, Angela wished for a fan. Her arms were heavy from a long day hammering in patches and scraping barnacles off the hull so the mighty Cantu could tar the seams and leaks. The man was bigger than any bouncer she'd ever seen, and Angela was thrilled he was a decent person. The crew mostly left her be, almost like she was one of them—respected, but otherwise kept at a distance and asked for help when needed. Reminded her of working with Marcos, which was a familiar relief, but she couldn't help but wonder about the raid and the armed soldiers. Something far outside her comfort zone.

Every time her stomach fluttered with nerves, her thoughts drifted back to the captain's sweet lips. A smile tugged at her lips. If only they'd had some privacy, Angela could've had her one night with a captain. Would one night be enough?

Not a chance.

She needed at least two to fix her itch—the good kind.

The ship creaked as the tide slowly crawled back, but so far only a few trivial leaks remained. Angela lifted a small board, blotting out the cone of fading daylight, and pinched a nail against it. Her tired arms relentlessly swung until the nail was flush—also of note, she didn't miss.

None of this felt like reality. She couldn't believe she'd actually fallen through time. How did it happen? Recalling her exact steps, Angela had entered the festival grounds with Emily. They'd waited in line and bought tickets for the ship tour. While waiting for the tour ship to open, Angela had insisted on shopping at the vendor tables, and the only thing she'd purchased...

Angela leaned down for another board, and the copper chain around her neck touched her chin. She straightened, and with a frown, her hand touched the amethyst. Could it be? Could this necklace have sent her back?

If she removed it, would she return to her time? And if so, where would she land? Since she slipped it over her head while on Lake Michigan and ended up in the middle of the Caribbean Sea, would taking it off in Cuba drop her somewhere far from land, helpless to the unforgiving ocean, or on a less friendly ship—perhaps an aircraft carrier? Uncertainty released the jewel back against her chest.

Angela climbed to the main deck to restock her small pile of boards.

"Ah, Angela, just who I was looking for." Captain Price's voice.

Angela turned, relief rushing through her, and she grinned. He was still so amazingly beautiful. Heat flushed up her chest, neck, and cheeks. She fanned herself with a small board. "Why's that?"

The captain pressed a gun into her hand. "Take this. I want you to have extra protection tonight."

Angela fought a recoil at the weapon. Despite its stunning craftsmanship and reflective beauty, it was a means of killing. She didn't like guns. "I can't take this."

"I insist."

"I don't know how to use it."

Captain Price smiled. "It's already loaded. You simply aim and squeeze. After all you've done so far, I think this shall be the simplest task you'll encounter. You need one of these, too." Captain Price slipped a short dagger off his belt and held it out to her.

She hesitated.

"For your safety, I insist," he repeated.

Angela accepted, finding a blade more practical for survival than a gun, and slipped it into her belt. The weight of weapons at her waist was foreign and uncomfortable. Coupled with her pouch—why she still carried her fried cell phone, she didn't know—the weight at her hips was going to leave her back sore in the morning. Regardless, she was still bringing her hammer—that was her security blanket.

"Daylight is falling. The rest of the raiding party awaits us. Let us go at once."

Nerves sloshed her stomach as Angela followed Captain Price off the ship. The crew staying behind moved swiftly to load the ship with all the provisions and supplies as Captain Price directed, preparing to set sail upon their return.

She crossed the soft sandy beach and into the green palms and ferns, where a small group of men chattered to themselves. All of them carried cutlasses and daggers at their belts, but only a couple had guns. Liverman inspected her loaded belt and frowned. She had one, and he didn't.

Angela fidgeted, wanting to give the man her gun if he'd drop that glare of hatred. Vallo's belt was lacking a gun as well. In the fading light, she saw guns and blades on Cantu and Buckley. Angela had been given special treatment over some of the crew, only dividing them further.

"Stay close, stay silent, and follow me," Captain Price addressed the party. "The hut is a thousand paces northeast by east."

That sounded far.

As if sensing her uneasiness, Captain Price grabbed her hand. "You can do this."

Her stomach knotted and twisted. Her hands trembled, but she nodded. The only way home was forward. The safest way home was by Captain Price's side.

Angela placed one foot in front of the other, gripping the captain firmly. The men mumbled behind them, but right now, she didn't care what they were saying.

In the fading sunset, wayward branches were harder to see. Angela ducked seconds too late, earning herself scratches on her cheek and shoulder. Her hand covered the sting and rubbed. Marching through endless soft sand burned her calves. She panted with the exertion and caught glimpses of the captain next to her, who never let her hand go, and his stamina was apparently much better than hers.

What else did he have excellent stamina for? Angela turned her sweeping gaze away and bit back a smile. He couldn't see her in the dimness, but she didn't want reaction noticed.

The men behind them skulked through the underbrush, refraining from arguments, jokes, or running commentary, surprisingly.

Captain Price pulled back on her hand. Angela stopped immediately. He whispered, "Just up ahead. Look about."

From behind a palm tree, Angela leaned, watching. Four armed men in uniform argued in front of a sad hut made of palm fronds. She listened to their Spanish. The syntax was different from what she was used to, but they'd found two bodies nearby, their own men. Price had said if they'd found the bodies, the pirates would be up against many more than a few soldiers. Their odds would be slim.

Angela asked, "Are we leaving now?"

"Why would we leave?" Captain Price asked, confused.

She was just as perplexed. "They found the two bodies from earlier. The other guards." She pointed toward the men as if he didn't understand where she got the information from.

"You speak Spanish?" Captain Price asked with astonishment.

"Don't you?" Angela was just as confused now.

"A few phrases and numbers, but nothing substantial. What else are they saying?"

Angela focused on the angry men and listened. "Two of the soldiers want to sound the alarm and wake the rest of the guards to scour the cove. The other two want to wait until the *Peibo del ler San Francisco* arrives so they can still effectively guard the hut. I think that's the name of a ship. I can't tell which pair are winning their case."

"A Spanish first-rate man-o'-war," Cantu said.

A shiver danced down her spine. "Uh, I think we should go. Finish the repairs and get out of here. No money is worth your life."

"And that's where you're wrong, my lady," Price said with a dark voice.

Angela frowned. The captain actually had a dollar value on his life? The greed of these men knew no bounds.

"What's going on up there?" Buckley asked.

"Four soldiers. Prepare to disable them and keep it quiet," Price said.

The men dragged swords from their belts.

"You can't be serious!" Angela whisper-yelled.

"You shouldn't be here, wench," Liverman said. "Do as you're told and stay quiet before you get us all killed."

"Stay by my side but out of swinging reach. You're far too valuable to lose." Over his shoulder, Captain Price said, "Go now!"

The men silently lurked closer, and Angela waited for all the pirates and their shiny weapons to move far enough away. When the four soldiers were engaged with the crew, Captain Price and the others entered the hut. Angela left the cover of the tree and followed them inside.

Barrels, like those in *Sea Lion*'s hold, were stacked all over. A few chests were among them. The men pried open lids with fervor.

"Furs," one man said.

"Sugarcane," another said.

"Tobacco," a third announced.

"Where's the treasure, Price?" Liverman asked.

"I know what I saw. It's here. I'm sure of it." Captain Price stretched his hand for Angela's hammer. He pried open another lid, and metal rattled. "Light! Give me light!"

A lantern was lit, and men leaned over the barrel. Eyes brightened and widened.

"What is it?" Angela asked and tilted her head out of the door, watching out for incoming threats.

The men snickered and cackled. The noises of excitement grew to laughter—true belly laughter. The men shouted in celebration.

"Load it up!" Captain Price ordered and gave Angela her hammer back. "Take it all!"

The men cheered, and with smooth cooperation she hadn't so far seen, the crew coordinated their efforts to carry out as many barrels as possible. Several more trips were necessary to get it all, but she noted the captain ordered them to take the gold coins first.

Angela stepped down from the hut, staying by the captain and Cantu, who shared a heavy load. This was silly. If she took a barrel, they'd move that much faster. Angela jogged back into the hut and shoved on the barrels until she found a lighter one. The furs. Hefting it over her shoulder, she quickly caught up.

"What in the devil's name are you doing?" Captain Price grunted.

"I'm helping."

"A lady doesn't work like a man!"

Pfft. "A lady who wants to get off this island and go home does."

Captain Price darted her a look, but he kept quiet.

The men of this time thought of women differently. Well, she was going to show the captain she wasn't useless, since all her hammering hadn't made it obvious.

Chapter 18

THE SEA LION, BATHED in eerie moonlight, floated at anchor ready to return to the seas. A longboat awaited just offshore with Hodgens and Riley set to receive, and the raiding crew one-by-one dropped their barrels of ill-gotten goods into the boat. Despite how lightweight the furs were, the barrel still ached on her shoulder. Angela waded into the saltwater and added her barrel. Her calves burned, and she rotated her shoulder to soothe it. What she wouldn't give for a bath, a fuzzy robe, a recliner, and a book.

Captain Price and Cantu heaved theirs over the low rail with metallic clinks of coins. She watched his backside as he exerted himself. Perhaps she'd skip everything after the bath if she could have a few hours with him. The warm fuzzies brought a smile to her face, but sharp arguing on the boat pulled her from the sweet daydream.

The captain was steaming angry, facing off against the quartermaster.

"We have enough treasure to split among us. We're on Spain's territory, on borrowed time. I insisted we must get underway," Riley said. His group lined the rail of the Sea Lion, awaiting orders from below. Couldn't these people ever get along?

"There's a hut full of goods unattended. We cannot just leave it. Never again shall we encounter such easy wealth," the captain said.

"We've lost too many men already. It's not worth the risk now. If we return to Nassau and add more men, we can succeed in taking the rest, after proper repairs are completed."

"The gold shall be gone by then. The *Peibo del ler San Francisco* is returning for it. It's now or never."

"I'm with the captain on this one," Liverman said, and everyone turned to him in surprise. "With double or treble the treasure, we shall never need to sail another day. Not one of us will ever find ourselves wanting for women, wine, or food ever again. It would be foolish to pass on it."

"I agree, too," Vallo piped up.

Buckley sighed. "I'm old. I have no need for more than we've already taken. But you young bucks deserve to live your lives like I never could. We go and we take it all. I just don't want to spend my final days in shackles or hanging from the gallows. I trust you, Captain, to make the right call for all of us, not just myself."

"I'm with the captain, too," Cantu said. "It's too easy to pass up. This could be our only chance. Instead of standing around arguing, we ought to return at once."

Quartermaster Riley folded his arms over his chest. "I don't like it, but I can't stop you. Take as much as you can carry. When you return, I'm setting sail, fully restored sails or not, even if that means I'm the new captain."

"Very brazen of you, Riley, but we shall be back. You keep this ship at the ready," Captain Price said.

Riley nodded and, together, he and Hodgens rowed their goods to the ship.

"We must hurry, men. Angela, since you can speak Spanish, I want you at my side again."

With the quartermaster at arms with the captain, she had even more reason to stay with Price. She'd never once thought of stopping the longboat for a ride to the *Sea Lion*.

The raiding crew made their way back into the cove, and Price and Angela moved slowly behind them, out of earshot. Price's jaw worked at some unknown stress. Was he worried Riley would take the partial treasure and leave without them?

Price had always been the level-headed leader, and seeing him in distress only caused her anxiety to boil over. Just like when she'd heard of her ailing mom's condition, Angela rushed into action.

"Hey," she said, gently touching his shoulder. "It's going to be okay."

Captain Price stopped and gazed into her eyes.

"Whatever happens next will be fine," she added. "You have a plan. We'll get through it, and when it's over, then decide the next steps."

He didn't reply, only studied her silently under the blue hue of the moon.

Angela repeated, "It's going to be okay."

Did she believe her own words? She'd spoken them so many times to her mom, mostly because the woman didn't remember Angela's previous attempts at comforting her, so for Angela, they were rote. True or not didn't matter; they weren't for her.

Worry lines creased the corners of his eyes. With a gentle finger, he tilted her chin up slightly. "No matter how grim the circumstances around you, no matter the threats to your life and safety or the strangeness of the world you landed in, you still offer to support me."

"I had practice," Angela said, dismissively.

Captain Price's features darkened. "You have a husband, and you never told me?"

Angela reached for his forearms and gripped him firmly. "I don't. My mom was sick. I cared for her."

Captain Price deflated. "My apologies for the err in judgment. I don't know much about the future, but if all women are as kind, skilled, and flexible as you, I welcome it's coming."

Angela squinted suspiciously. "What do you know of the future?"

The lines softened. "Enough to know that as much as I welcome your arrival, I fear constantly for you. A curse, if you will."

"I'm a curse?" Angela asked, taken aback. She released him. "I'm a burden to you?"

"Well, yea, technically."

Angela flinched at the stinging words.

He leaned closer. "You're a burden I would gladly accept a hundred times over on my worst day, through squalls, droughts, and fair winds. I owe you a great debt of gratitude, and couldn't imagine my life had I not met you. It truly might have ceased already."

Angela's heart thumped in her ears, and her chest warmed. Did he just say what she thought he said? Too much seawater was making her hear things.

Captain Price collected her hands and squeezed. "Angela, you are my angelfish. If I knew the men weren't peeping, I'd ask you to kiss me, but it's too risky right now, and my plan is falling apart before we can even finish repairs on the *Sea Lion*." Price headed toward the remaining raiders, and Angela kept stride, pushing brush out of their faces.

Angela thought he only wanted another trip or two's worth of gold from the hut and sail away to safety. "What plan is that?"

"That gold was only to appease the crew. I need them to assist me in a task I know they shall not volunteer for, but now I can't even get them to agree to want the rest of the gold."

"Why do they need to want the gold?"

"I made a promise to my brother."

Angela's eyes widened with interest. "For what?"

The captain shifted aside a frond and exhaled. "My brother and I enlisted in the Royal Navy, as our father had and his before him. The sea was all we knew. But the world isn't the same anymore. We suffered with insufficient and sometimes skipped rations, and little to no pay. If any of us spoke up, we were given lashes." He paused and shook his head. "Every time the cat came out of the bag, we all held our breaths and quelled our panic."

"Cat? Is this another real cat?" Angela recalled the feline's escape from the sinking ship.

"Cat-o'-nine-tails. A whip for punishment. It's something you never forget: the quick snap of the lines, the stinging heat of the tears in your flesh, and the warm trickle of your own blood. Cry out and the captain counts extra just for his own pleasure. So when Wilcox and the *Sea Lion* approached, hoisting the black, our captain's fear showed on his face, and we all silently rejoiced. The captain took his own lashings that day, and my brother and I joined the pirates. The promise of freedom was too great to resist, and the riches were a bonus."

"Sounds like becoming a pirate was good for you." Better than the alternative, anyway.

"I never intended to continue as long as I have. We were restocking near Port Royal when a Spanish man-o'-war anchored off shore, and my brother, the brazen dolt, offered his life so we could flee, and that day I made him a promise I cannot break."

The captain had saved her life many times—from the sinking ship to the overzealous crew, and she wanted to do this. "I want to help you keep your promise."

"And that, my lady, makes you the finest woman I've ever met." Price found her hand and held her tight.

No one else had treated her like such an equal, trusting her so fully. Brandon Spindleton, with his idiotic and immature blackmail scheme and a team of attorneys at the ready for vengeance, was not a man compared to Captain Henry Price. She'd finally found a man worth his salt.

Angela smiled. She wanted to feel his heat, to explore his body, and caress his skin. But there was never enough time or privacy. She ached to touch him, to climb aboard his sexy body and drive him like a forklift.

"Are you ready to translate for me?" Price asked.

Of all the things she'd done lately, that would be the easiest—but not the most fun. She'd forgotten to ask what the promise to his brother was exactly, but it didn't matter. Some things were meant to stay private.

"Let's do this."

19

Chapter 19

In sight of their target, Price gestured for his men to take refuge behind the trees and watch for an updated count on the guards. They likely had more men on alert, but Price brought more too. For a second, he worried how she would handle this. Being from the future of kind and caring people, he couldn't imagine Angela would keep herself level watching men fight to the death.

And this wouldn't be an honorable, fair fight.

He pulled Angela against his chest until her scent filled his nose. He closed his eyes and breathed her in deep, wishing he could do something else deeply. Upholding his promise to his brother would break his promise to Angela. Leading her into the fray deliberately put her in harm's way. Price's insides twisted. His resolve faltered, and his heart fluttered.

This was not a situation to take lightly. Price never did, but suddenly it felt tremendously heavier. He whispered, "I don't know what the outcome shall be, but I want you to know..." he trailed off, unable to voice his fears.

"What is it?" she whispered.

The skies through the canopy lightened just slightly, threatening the coming of dawn. The Sea Lion would part from this island soon. Time was almost up. "Stay close."

Price couldn't see anyone near the hut. He gestured for the crew to approach, and they all crept forward into the clearing, alert for an ambush. Price led Angela and a couple others inside the hut, while Vallo and the rest waited as lookouts.

Captain Price pushed barrels and chests until he found a light one. He offered it to Angela, still annoyed she strained herself on his account, but maybe her cooperation and effort shall earn her leniency with the crew. So if he failed to return to the *Sea Lion*, the crew might treat her with a shred of dignity.

He could only hope.

Price collected barrels and passed them along until everyone's arms were full. Satisfied with their take, he and Angela exited behind the others.

Instead of an orderly and efficient line of men rushing back to the ship, he found Liverman standing next to his barrel, and a pistol pointed at Price. The rest of the men stopped when they noticed. Several dropped their burdens and glanced at each other, wondering what to do. Angela wisely stayed behind him.

Fury surged within Price. "What's the meaning of this, Liverman?"

The smirking traitor said, "Since you trained your loyalties on the wench, we sit fit to dispatch you as captain. Anyone who disagrees, I shall duel them at once."

Cantu and Buckley stared in disbelief, and Vallo approached Liverman's shoulder. This is exactly what Price didn't need at this moment, but he trusted Vallo to make the right move.

"Is this your decision?" Vallo asked Liverman, slipping a pistol from his sash and holding at his side.

"With certainty, just as I expect your support, my friend." Liverman kept the pistol aimed at Price's chest. "Since none of you are short of wits enough to fight me, then I declare the treasure and the *Sea Lion* are now under my control."

No one made a move, not even Cantu or Hodgens, as expected. Most of the crew were content in their roles and preferred to ignore the politics of the sea, but Price shot a glare at Vallo. He'd expected the man to keep a closer eye on the agitator, not encourage him.

"You brought this upon yourself." Vallo leveled the pistol at Price too.

Price's lips parted, his brow furrow. Liverman's betrayal was expected, truthfully, but Vallo's, that was a devastating blow. They'd had a deal. Vallo was supposed to stay undercover with the agitators and feed information back to Price. He was also supposed to manipulate their traitorous speak and prevent exactly this.

It couldn't have come at a worse time.

With a smug smirk, Liverman loosened his guard. Vallo abruptly swung his arm at Liverman. Before the traitor responded, Vallo squeezed the trigger. A single blast rocked the sleepy island. Angela gasped and gripped the back of Price's tunic. Birds fluttered from the trees, and the men flinched from the noise. Liverman grasped his chest and collapsed, mouth gaped open like a fish.

Price blinked and smiled in relief. For a moment there, he was truly worried. "Thank you, friend."

Vallo nodded and returned the smile.

Price gently urged Angela out from behind him. "It's over now. The last of the thorns in my side has been vanquished. Let us return to the ship with our prize."

Angela shot him a look of disbelief. "You set this up from the beginning?"

"I must maintain relationships to protect my standing." Price labored too long and hard to give up everything for a couple of men with selfish ambitions.

"I... I can't believe this. A thief and a murderer? And here I thought Brandon was a piece of shi..." Angela met the eyes of the pirates around her and trailed off.

Price touched her arm. "I can explain better once we are safely aboard the ship. Spain is lurking in this jungle, and we are standing here with their treasure. I insist we move at once."

Candlelight flickered through the brush, just beyond the darkness, catching his attention. Price stiffened at the indecipherable voices. The soldiers were returning. They were way too close, and at this distance, the crew couldn't outrun them—with or without their arms full.

Angela turned to the captain. "They're here. There's someone here."

Regret was a funny thing. Sometimes it was there, teasing on the horizon. Other times it popped up unexpectedly, like a startled jackrabbit. Right now, the horizon soared toward him at unimaginable speeds. He only hoped the next few minutes didn't reveal the jackrabbit.

Cantu whispered, "Men incoming!"

Pistols would draw plenty of attention, but when those soldiers spotted the crew, they'd open fire. Vallo scrambled to reload. Another man picked up Liverman's unspent pistol. Cantu and McKee had theirs drawn and ready. Everyone added a sword to their empty hands.

Soldiers emerged from the brush into the clearing, surrounding them, but it was Vallo's weapon once again trained on Price that stilled Price's hand.

Boom. The startled jackrabbit popped up.

Chapter 20

WHEN ANGELA WAS YOUNGER, she learned quickly to avoid social media. She had too many personal issues to deal with, and she didn't want to be inundated with useless epithets from people who didn't truly care about her struggles—not to mention the Spindleton's privacy requirements. She'd found the drama at times could be more harmful than supportive. Words were powerful—dangerous when used wrong and had the potential to kill.

But a pistol in someone's face made social media feel…insignificant. Artificial. Cowardly. Angela knew what the captain needed right now, and even with a pistol in the face of her only ally, Angela stepped forward, shoulder to shoulder at Price's side in solidarity. She was no longer the only one hated by the crew, but she didn't understand why they kept turning on the captain. All he wanted was to lead them toward the treasure they wanted while he upheld a promise to his brother. It made no sense.

"Captain, I cannot allow such nonsense to continue," Vallo said with a self-satisfied smirk and addressed everyone. "In this, I must apologize. In the essence of truth, you don't know of your captain's true objective, so hear me all. Price planned to destroy the *Peibo del ler San Francisco*."

Amid the gasps, Angela faced the captain. He thought they could best a first-rate man-o'-war? The ship carrying a small army he'd already admitted would be impossible to defeat? All in the name of wealth and riches? Angela exhaled slowly to calm her fury. She still had to contend with an angry armed man and a handful of Spaniards with stern faces and bayonet blades attached to their muskets, clearly not understanding much.

Vallo continued, clearly enjoying this. "No one is arguing the hunter's merit of retrieving recovered Spanish gold, but using it as a bribe is beyond even your integrity. Sending the crew to slaughter a warship full of Spaniard soldiers is even worse. *Capitán* Delgado was only doing his job. If you had done yours, you wouldn't be in this mess."

Price tensed next to her.

"Why not ask the crew to jump overboard and drown? The end result ought to be the same. So I did what any well-meaning sailor would do to save his crew: I called upon Spain and disclosed your petty plan of vengeance. In exchange for your life, the crew shall be allowed their freedom."

The other crewmen murmured their shock and disbelief, and Angela's mouth gaped open. This whole ruse was for *revenge*? Angela's vision narrowed, and her chest ached. She pressed a fist against her heart as a flash of the betrayal from Brandon and his scheme loosened her knees.

Once again, she'd been used and betrayed.

After everything she'd shared with Captain Price, he'd withheld the devastating truth from her. He was using her to exact vengeance. The kisses were fake. The help he'd asked of her was for his own selfish gain—repair the *Sea*

Lion to take on a warship, translate the Spanish for their upper hand.

Tears flooded her eyes as history repeated itself. She couldn't face Captain Price. Angela darted away into the jungle.

"*Recuperarla!*" a man barked orders to retrieve her.

"Angela!" Captain Price shouted, voice thick with panic.

Pain tore through her. Angela ran harder, slapping branches and slicing her hands on thick leaves. She sobbed and stumbled, landing on her knees and burying her hands in more sand. So much sand! She was tired of being filthy, sticky, sandy. Sand was in areas it didn't belong, irritating her skin and making her wish for a hot shower. With angry knees, Angela got up and dusted her hands off. She ran. Branches stung her face, but she couldn't stop.

Where could she go? The men on the ship all wanted her killed—or worse. Even if she pleaded her case for help, would they bother? It was a suicide mission! Would the *Sea Lion* even still be there?

Instead, Angela could head toward the interior of the island, pretend to be a lost local, and use Spanish as her first language again. But she was rusty, and the people here spoke differently from what she was used to. Why would they help her? She had no money or useful skills. It wasn't like she expected to find a ship repair shop and apply for a position.

Angela tripped again and rested on her hands and knees, panting. The necklace swung in front of her face, bumping her chin.

When she'd purchased her necklace at the Tall Ships festival, she remembered the old woman saying, 'These *powerful gems have been known to grant your truest desire while protecting you from bad humors, so be careful how you use them.'*

If putting the necklace on brought her here, in theory, removing it would take her home. Brandon's destruction of her social life was nothing compared to being used by dozens of men or killed. In that case, she wished to return home. She had friends who meant more to her than anything, especially Emily. She had extended family she hadn't seen in a while, and a job she loved, and coworkers she adored.

Angela wished she were somewhere safe, warm, and happy. She wasn't going to find any of that here—except for the warm, but warm wasn't the same as hot, humid, and sticky.

Angela fisted the necklace and lifted it off her head. It snagged in her nest of hair. She pulled harder, tearing hair with it. She sniffled and looked around. Nothing changed. She didn't feel anything. Was she in Cuba but in her time or was she still in the past?

Angela stuffed the necklace into her pocket and stood, dusting off her knees. What she wouldn't give for a cheeseburger and a chocolate milkshake. She wiped her face, and a cold metal tube pressed against the back of her head.

She'd never been held at gunpoint, but Angela was certain that was a gun. Angela sucked in a breath and held out her hands in surrender. Either she was the unluckiest woman in the world, or she was still in the past. Did that also qualify for unluckiest?

"*No se mueva*," he'd ordered her to stay still. His hand retrieved the blade tucked into her rope belt. Then he tugged free her pistol, which she wouldn't have used, anyway. When she'd darted off into the woods, she'd forgotten about the hammer left by the hut. Now she had no means of defense.

"*Vamos*." He pushed the barrel into her head, sparking pain, forcing her to move one foot in front of the other.

"*Más rápido ahora, mujer.*"

His annoyed tone was clear, but she had no reason to move faster. She was a coward, just like her father, abandoning people when they were needed most. The sooner she returned to the group, the sooner they'd kill her. But she wasn't one of them, only a tool to be used. Tears returned.

Angela walked back with a gun pressed to her skull. In the small clearing around the hut, the soldiers had trained guns on each of the *Sea Lion* crew. She didn't want to look at Captain Price, but also worried for him. The captain's pain was clear on his face. What had they done to him? She couldn't see any new injuries, but that didn't mean he wasn't hurt. Holding her chin high, Angela focused on the faces of her captors.

"*Llevamos a la mujer también*," the man behind her said in a gleeful tone. Soldiers cackled and smiled. The man gripped her arm and shoved her forward. Angela landed painfully on her knees in the sand. Didn't take a genius to figure what they had in mind.

Vallo watched with that same smirk on his stupid face. One of the soldiers approached the weasel, and together they spoke Spanish fluently. Vallo asked to keep some treasure for his efforts. The guards allowed him to take one barrel and leave, expecting messages of any new developments on the *Sea Lion*, like he was some hired spy.

Vallo nodded and said to the crew, "Good luck with Spain's noose. I hear it's quite disagreeable." He cackled and left, disappearing into greens with a barrel of gold in his arms.

"*Los llevamos todos,*" another Spaniard soldier said. He waved his gun, urging all the crew to set off toward their fate, including Angela.

The purple and pinks in the sky shifted into yellows and oranges, lighting the worn path leading away from the hut. A pair of soldiers started off, leading the way, followed by one soldier per pirate. The one who'd chased her lifted her up and shoved her forward. She had no chance to steal her hammer back.

Marching through the scratchy undergrowth, Angela swatted at bugs and scratched at bites. Streaks of blood covered her hands. Her cheek still stung. But none of that mattered if they intended to hang her. After all their deep-throated chuckles, she figured they had other things in mind first. Angela ducked under a low-lying branch, and the soldier behind her shoved her shoulder. She couldn't believe this was reality.

As the captain, Price was somewhere near the front of the line. Angela couldn't see him. She didn't want to see him. All she'd ever wanted was a man who respected her, and treated her like an equal, and included her in his life, among his friends. She'd thought Captain Price met those desires.

He'd kept secrets from her—secrets that changed everything.

He'd kept her safe—only to use her in other ways.

And the crew hated her—wanted her dead or worse.

She had been wrong on all counts, and her necklace wouldn't get her out of here.

Angela swiped her forehead with her tunic, wishing for rain. After hiking for what felt like an hour, the jungle cleared to a beach and a shallow cove. Anchored just out of the cove, out of sight of the *Sea Lion*, was a massive warship with multiple decks of cannon ports, and directly behind it was a smaller ship—very different from theirs.

A lump settled in her throat while they were all forced into a longboat. Angela climbed in last. For the briefest second, she met Captain Price's eyes.

She thought real concern was there. For himself or for her and the crew?

The soldiers rowed them to the hull of the warship. Angela read the name painted on the back and shivered. *Peibo del ler San Francisco.* And a second, smaller ship was behind it, as if the warship didn't have enough power on its own, but she couldn't find the name.

Captain Price lived with the burden of regret for so long, he'd become accustomed to its heft on his shoulders, never imagining it could crush him entirely.

Then she appeared.

This angel had dropped onto his deck and saved his life. Keeping her secure against the crew was a challenge he hadn't planned on, but he persevered. She was his sign to give up the sea life and take her to the mainland to live out their lives in peace.

Just like his old friend Eric Lemoine.

Captain Price never wanted to fail at his promise to William Price, but when he did, he planned take his enemy with him—that was realistically where he'd find his peace. All the while, Price had primed Noah Riley to take over the ship, and Riley succeeded. The quartermaster followed the rules and kept the crew's focus toward the right goals. And as a show of strength, Riley had threatened to take ownership of the crew if they didn't return. Everything was set.

But over their short time together, Angela switched from burden to gift, and he'd made a grave mistake. Instead of turning his back on the men and embracing the gift, stubborn Price had to rally his cause. She was his hope the insurmountable plan could succeed at all, and he'd blindly rushed headfirst into it.

That hope was gone.

As they approached the warship, he realized now, far too late, avenging his brother's murder was a waste of his life. The dead no longer cared about their business. The dead only cared their loved ones lived full, happy lives. In that, Price had failed his brother, also.

As the longboat rowed them to their deaths, the most beautiful, strong, and courageous woman he'd ever met was going to die right along with him, all because he couldn't choose her first.

If he could give it all up, hold her in his arms, tell her how he felt, and beg her to stay with him, he'd do it. He'd do it without thinking twice. But she didn't want him. He saw the look of horror on her face, and that was after she'd declared she wanted to go home, and he promised her safe passage home. Now he couldn't keep that promise, either.

Once in a lifetime did a woman appear on a ship who saved a man's life, fixed his ship, and showed him life had more meaning than he could see. His thoughtless mission would cause her death. An innocent. A woman who deserved so much more. He was too blind to see it before it was too late.

Always too late.

Just like with William.

I'm sorry I failed you, brother.

I'm sorry I failed you, my angel.

Price would always be a failure.

Chapter 21

AT ANOTHER URGING FROM a gun barrel, Angela stood up inside the wobbly longboat and climbed the hull of the *Peibo del ler San Francisco*. On the main deck, about two dozen armed Spaniard soldiers stood around her with snarls on their clean faces and adorned muskets aimed at her. Angela's hands went up in surrender. The rest of the captured *Sea Lion* crew settled in around her, but they didn't raise their hands.

Cantu was stoic and standing tall, but Buckley's face was showing downright terror. Vallo was nowhere to be seen, not surprising.

Angela hoped Captain Price was behind her.

The guards who caught them climbed aboard and spoke to the others in Spanish, explaining the pirates had murdered the guards and stolen from King Philip V. One of the soldiers asked why a pirate crew had a woman and what they were going to do with her. Another man grinned and wagged his brows. Angela swallowed a thick lump caught in her throat. But he was quickly elbowed by the soldier next to him.

A gangly and weathered man in a fine uniform pushed through the gaggle of armed soldiers, clearly their leader. The soldiers addressed him as *Capitán* Delgado, who at once brushed by Angela and approached Captain Price with a confident swagger and a nasty smirk. Angela exhaled deeply knowing Captain Price was behind her, but nerves returned when a pair of soldiers fastened their grips on Captain Price's upper arms—restraining him. Based on Captain Price's set jaw and furrowed brow, restraint was needed.

Capitán Delgado's spoken English was heavily accented. "Henry Price, we meet again, and I see not under better circumstances."

Captain Price lifted his chin to the taller man, neck muscles tense. "*Captain* Henry Price, if you will."

Capitán Delgado snorted in derision. "You thought you could escape with gold belonging to King *Felipe*?" His condescending tone elicited chuckles in his ranks. "Not only shall you *not* escape my clutches again, but when the tide returns, *Peibo del ler San Francisco* will sink your little *Sea Lion* back to the bottom of the ocean where it belongs, and any pirates who fall with it are merely a bonus for the Crown."

Captain Price struggled in the guards' grips, and Delgado smirked and strolled along his other captives. Facing Angela he stopped. Dark pools of evil deviously raked over her body. Angela recoiled.

"Leave her out of this! She has nothing to do with our business!" Captain Price shouted with fear in his voice.

"Oh, it's far too late for that," Delgado said.

Captain Price struggled harder, true terror and fear on his fine features. "Angela! Listen to me, Angela! I'm beyond words of gratitude for all you have shown me. I'm an imbecile for choosing a past I can't change over a future I didn't know I wanted. I cannot properly convey how much despair these unfortunate circumstances have caused me. But it's not too late for you. Angela, you belong back home, in your own time."

Angela flinched. *He knew?* That was why he'd never questioned her strange costume in a bag or her mention of GPS or any other modern technology. He never questioned her sanity. In fact, when she was questioning her own, he was reassuring her everything was real. *He knew.* Regardless of her million new questions, the most important was clear: Captain Price cared about her. He pulled forward against his captors, trying to reach her, but it was no use. Tears pricked at her eyes. Angela stayed in place, hands raised in surrender, but she desperately wanted to rush to his side.

She wanted to tell him just how much she cared too.

Delgado watched with amusement as Price continued his plea, sounding more like a sorrowful goodbye filled with desperation. "I was blind! Blind by the desire to seek justice in the name of my brother. I know now how foolish I was, but it's too late for me. Spain shall have its ceremony. Go home. Save yourself."

His thoughtful apology was just what her heart needed to hear, but the goodbye ripped her to shreds. Angela stifled her sob and blinked back the tears flooding her eyes.

"Please, *Capitán* Delgado, I beg of you. Spare Angela. Set her free, and I promise full cooperation."

She didn't know how to go home, but she'd take her freedom.

"How charming," Delgado said, dismissively. "Ortega, retrieve the gallows at once. Spain shall not wait another day for justice against these uncivilized cretins."

The first mate rushed away. Now? They were going to hang Captain Price and the crew *now*? This could not be happening. No, no, please no. Angela had to do something. The Spaniard hadn't agreed to release her, and if he killed the whole *Sea Lion* crew, there was no hope for her.

"Let us go," Angela ordered in English with controlled emotion in her voice.

The warship soldiers remained stoic, ignoring her plea. *Capitán* Delgado rubbed his smooth jaw.

Without her captain, she had nothing left to lose. She'd do whatever it took to save his life...again.

"*Libéranos*," Angela repeated herself in Spanish, more firmly this time, eliciting chuckles and mumbles from the soldiers.

Capitán Delgado lifted her hand and kissed her knuckles. "We have not formally met," he said in Spanish. "I am *Capitán* Delgado. I must know the name of the lovely face before me."

"Keep your hands off her, Delgado. This has nothing to do with her," Captain Price said, straining against the arms holding him.

Angela wrenched her hand free with a fake smile on her face. "You don't care about my name, and I don't care about yours. Let us go."

Delgado frowned at her flippant demand, but desperation had her saying things she'd never consider before, especially lying, especially to the authorities. She added, "We meant you no harm. The man responsible for the affront to the Spanish Crown was Vallo. As I understand, he worked for you."

Capitán Delgado straightened and smoothed his button-lined coat. "Not a simple woman, I see. I usually have a use for women, but that mouth of yours shall become a problem."

Jerk. But she could work with that. in Spanish, she said, "Then we agree, having me—us—out of your hair will prevent problems. Allow us to leave, and this burden on you will be no longer."

Delgado lifted his lips as if an idea sprang to mind. Ignoring her plea, he strolled back to Captain Price. "She means something to you, correct?" A vicious smile split his lips.

"Please, I beg of you, free her. I shall turn over all the gold taken and return for the punishment you see fit, but I beg you... Please." Captain Price's distraught eyes broke her heart. Price couldn't see a way out of this, and he was willing to give his life to preserve hers. For all the injustice, for all Price's suffering and fear, she wanted to attack Delgado in fury, but she couldn't. Her stomach knotted and her hands trembled. She hated to feel useless.

"Garcia," the enemy captain said, "show the woman our lovely accommodations below deck, while I spend some quality time with our prisoners."

Fury roared through her, but she didn't know how to stop any of this. The blade Captain Price had given her had been confiscated. The hammer had been left by the hut. She packed a mean punch when she needed to, but that wouldn't get her far with a deck full of armed soldiers.

Garcia's hands gripped her arms, and he shoved her forward to the ladder. With a last look at Captain Price, whose withdrawn face of despair crushed her, she wrenched her arms out of the man's grip and climbed down the ladder with her dignity.

Shafts of light from the sunrise through the portholes illuminated squares on the floor. Into the dank underbelly of the massive ship, Angela allowed her eyes to adjust, and the soldiers behind her forced her forward and down another ladder, and another. With each step lowering her further and further under the waterline, the light went out. A twinge of claustrophobia reared its head.

One man lit a lantern behind her and told her to turn left, and having no other choice, Angela obeyed. Where they were taking her couldn't be a bedroom.

Was that a relief or a bigger fear?

Angela stopped at a closed door. The soldier with the light unlocked it, and the door creaked open. He carried the light inside, and Garcia shoved her forward. Iron bars cut the stifling, stench-filled room in half. Chains were anchored to the walls and floors like marionette lines. One man in chains slumped over on the floor. Others leaned against the back wall, still like death. They may as well have been dead.

Sure didn't smell alive.

The first soldier unlocked the iron bars, and Garcia shoved her through. The doors screamed as they clanked shut behind her, and the soldier locked the door. "Stay in the brig until the captain is ready for you," Garcia told her in Spanish.

Angela held the sticky bars in her hands and blinked back tears from the strong urine stench.

Would she ever see Captain Price again?

Chapter 22

ORTEGA AND ANOTHER SOLDIER carried an armful of hangman's nooses and climbed the ratlines. One at a time, the men dropped them over the boom and secured them. Their faces glistened from the exertion. Price wished all the discomfort possible on these vile men. At gunpoint, his crew solemnly awaited the fate expected by all pirates.

But Angela didn't deserve this end.

She didn't deserve whatever was happening below deck. Picturing the enemy attacking her while she cried out in horror, fury sparked in his veins, powering the urge to fight, but even if he and the crew broke free from the Spaniards, the aimed guns would end their endeavor before they reached the companionway.

He was not leaving this ship without Angela.

Capitán Delgado settled at a small table, and a petty officer retrieved tea and paperwork for him. When the nooses were lashed around the boom, the soldiers lined up wood crates to finish the makeshift gallows. Satisfied, Delgado nodded to the men restraining Price, and he was released. The muskets remained, ready to fire.

Price flexed his shoulders and exchanged glances with his crew. Cantu kept his chin held high, while Buckley appeared distraught at his worst fear manifesting. He couldn't focus on his many regrets. Price couldn't see a way out of this, but he had to keep his eyes open, just in case. For Angela, he couldn't give up.

"First set of men, please." *Capitán* Delgado sipped from his teacup.

Price wanted to shove the porcelain through the captain's teeth. "Where is our trial? The Piracy Act of 1698 states we are entitled to a trial to determine guilt."

Delgado set down his cup and saucer and licked his lips. He spoke as if reciting from rote memory. "If delivering the accused to such a place for questioning about their piracies and robberies is too much trouble, acts of piracy can be examined, tried, and adjudged in any place at sea." He grinned deviously. "Even I read England's amended statue dated the year of our lord, 1700. Since you are English, I am following your laws rightfully, not that I must."

Price gritted his teeth. "The statue also states that a commissioner calls a court of admiralty consisting of at least seven people voting in said court."

Delgado tilted his head in contemplation. "If that is your wish, so be it. Men! Our pirate here requires a guilty verdict of his capital crimes before his conscience can accept his rightful death. All in favor of guilty, raise your hand!"

Every Spaniard soldier on deck lifted his hand. Bastards.

Price ran a hand down his face. He needed more time to think. "And of Angela? She is not a pirate. Let her go!"

The Spaniard captain sipped from his cup and uncorked his inkwell. "The woman in your crew, at a minimum, is guilty by assisting acts of piracy. She was witnessed with stolen goods in her hands."

"She was pressed. She's innocent," Price countered.

Ignoring the desperate plea, Delgado gestured for his soldiers to commence the hanging, while dipping his quill in the ink.

"Too late for begging and bargaining," *Capitán* Delgado said with boredom.

Obediently, soldiers stepped forward and threatened four of his crew to obey at gunpoint, including Buckley. The fear twisting the old man's face crushed Price. He was a good man, an experienced old salt, even if his eyesight failed him on occasion. Knowing the man would prefer instant death at the hands of his own crew rather than the enemy, Price couldn't do anything to save him from his worst nightmare.

This was all Price's fault.

Four men were stopped with their toes touching their own crates, just under the boom. All but Buckley stepped onto the crates before them. The carpenter refused, and his disobedience earned him a sharp jab in the back. Buckley stepped up, and the soldiers fastened his men's hands securely with rope.

No man deserved this humiliation. All their deaths would be on his conscience.

"You cannot use English law as an excuse to deal out your own vengeance," Price said, hoping to delay the captain's next orders with a plea for fairness.

"Your pathetic ship attempted to take the *Peibo del ler San Francisco* as a prize. My father's ship, my ship. You all should've been hanging at the gallows for it, but my father, rest his soul, was too kind for a captain. I have no such qualms. This punishment is long overdue. Be thankful for the extra time you had and didn't deserve."

"Most of this crew is new. They're innocent."

"No one's innocent the moment they step foot on that ship."

That was it. No more negotiating. Delgado wouldn't see reason and didn't understand mercy. Price shouldn't have been surprised.

The *Sea Lion*, with a stolen Spanish banner at her masthead, had been hunting a prize off the coast of Hispaniola. The *Peibo del ler San Francisco*, indeed, a first-rate man-o'-war, surprised them and hailed for communication. Too close to flee and vastly underpowered, the Sea Lion had no chance of survival.

Captain Lemoine had decided to send a man to distract the enemy. William Price had volunteered. William agreed the moment he cleared the rail, the *Sea Lion* was to immediately leave while he put on his best show, or his sacrifice would've been for naught. Price had argued with his brother, and the shouts heard around the ships. Spain became suspicious. Captain Lemoine had told William to go at once or their plan was wasted.

William went.

Unwilling to let such selflessness go and unable to part from his brother, Henry Price followed.

The *Sea Lion* had shifted forward, gliding, hoping to make range before further suspicions were raised. But the plan had been a failure.

"William Price and I tried to negotiate with you. We meant you no harm," Captain Price said, trying one last approach for mercy.

Delgado looked up from his writing. "Your brother claimed he had was hunting a pirate ship with stolen porcelain bound for England. And that such goods had left this very island."

"That's how I remember it, yea."

Delgado set down his quill. "Cuba never exported porcelain, and your banner was stolen. Spanish merchants and naval ships know the proper condition our banner must maintain, and yours was in near tatters. Such shame! Your brother lied, and I simply challenged his word. At that, he was afraid. A little mouse, so knowing nothing else, he attacked me in a panic. My father took leniency on you both, and accepted his deal to free you, knowing one captured pirate was more valuable than whatever stolen goods the *Sea Lion* truly had on board. When the tale of William Price's cowardice and surrender reached the *Boston News-Letter*, damaging the pirate reputation, the black banner would no longer instill terror on the seas."

Price stared at the Spaniard, dumbfounded. He'd never read the story.

Delgado retrieved his quill and dipped it. "I would've hanged you. Better late than never, as they say."

Price had leaped to the *Sea Lion* before it was out of range, believing his own skill had led to his escape. All these years, Captain Price had carried such guilt, plotted with all the spare energy he had, hoping for the opportunity to lay waste to this ship and everyone on board, because he was strong enough. He was capable. He was cunning. And he'd shouted over the rail a promise to avenge William Price's sacrifice.

His brother had simply made a deal.

Price moved to strike. If he couldn't prevent any of their deaths, he could take one of the enemies with him, and he knew just the man. A sharp pain struck the back of his knee, and Price fell to the deck. A cold metal barrel of a musket was pressed against his neck, and the glinting blade of the bayonet stretched just past his face.

Delgado scratched the pen on parchment. "The official documents shall list your death as…accidental. And such an untimely mishap prevented your crew from receiving their due justice."

The flippant use of 'due justice' only infuriated Price, but showing anger wouldn't help. "Is there anything I may offer in bargain for Angela's life? She is an innocent in all this. You've taken a deal once, do it again."

Delgado gestured to his men again, and the soldiers slipped nooses over the *Sea Lion*'s crewmen. Delgado set his pen down and approached Price with loose arms at his sides. "The only thing I want from you is your long overdue death."

In a flash, *Capitán* Delgado unsheathed a short blade from his backside and stabbed Price discreetly in the abdomen and slid the blade out clean.

Mouth gaped open in surprise, Price stumbled back and covered the wound. The blade was short enough to cause a higher chance of suffering than death, but the wound was unfortunate.

"On my count," Delgado ordered, "swing the boom starboard over the deck. Allow their bowels and bladders to empty into the sea as they hang to their deaths."

Price inhaled a shaky breath. If torturing him and his crew was of no consequence, what did *Capitán* Delgado have in mind for Angela?

23

Chapter 23

Cutting onions was like a gentle lake breeze compared to the vapors down here. And she thought the *Sea Lion* had been awful. Urine, feces, sweat, vomit, and who knew what else stung her eyes. Angela pulled at the sticky iron bars, but they didn't give. She reached for the lock, but it was welded to the cage, and there was no obvious latch. She was trapped in the guts of a warship during a time in history she should've only read about in a textbook.

Emily would've had a field day with this insanity. Angela? Not so much. She didn't belong here. Good thing Robin didn't show up on time. Robin would've struggled so much worse with all this lawlessness.

Groans and a rattle of chain turned her head. A filthy, stringy-haired man leaned against the bulwark. He tilted his face up to hers, and a shaggy beard covered most of his face. He looked to be in his forties, and far from prime health. Other men in similar condition were chained to the wall and floor nearby. Clearly Delgado didn't take care of his prisoners very well. Looking at the men made Angela ache for a shower, and the cheeseburger craving returned.

"A companion in the hold," the stringy-haired man said with awe. By his accent, he was English. "And a woman at that. How quaint. Never expected the Spaniards to be so generous. If this is the delusion of a dying man, I welcome it."

"You're not delusional, but if you try anything..." Angela trailed off her warning. The shackles made her warning useless.

The stringy-haired man chuckled. "You must be real. Come sit. Give a tired man's neck a break."

Angela sat on the floor near the man, but out of chain reach. Since she couldn't change the horrible events above them, conversation was a welcome distraction. "What did you do to land yourself in here?"

Her chatty fellow prisoner pushed hair out of his face. "I tried to do the right thing. The more interesting question plaguing me is what did *you* do?"

Angela reflected on the exact cause that brought her aboard and cringed. "I helped pirates steal Spanish gold."

His shaggy brows lifted, and he grinned. "Is that so? Then I'd say your rightful place is here by me. For the sake of my otherwise mundane endless hours in this cell, what great ship did you sail upon? It deserves recognition."

"The *Sea Lion*."

The prisoner blinked once then twice, silently staring.

"The *Sea Lion*," she repeated louder.

"I heard you. I just cannot believe you. The *Sea Lion* is outside this hull right now? Is that what you're telling me?"

"Not exactly. It's—" Angela pointed in the rough direction she thought it was "—somewhere over there. We're still repairing the storm damage. The rigging's a mess, last I saw."

Interesting that she referred to the crew as *we*.

"The *Sea Lion* is...is here?"

"Yes." Angela frowned. This guy's company was quickly becoming less enjoyable than she'd hoped.

"Who else is on this ship? Your mates? Who are they?" The eagerness in his voice was strange. He must know the crew.

"Cantu and Buckley are up there. A bunch of men too, but I don't know their names. And—"

A gleam of excitement lit his eyes. "What about the quartermaster?"

"Riley is on the *Sea Lion*. He was in charge of getting ready to escape. He's probably going to leave us behind now." That was a depressing thought, but that was the instruction. Leave before the *Sea Lion* was caught too.

"No, no no." His hand slashed at the air in frustration. "Price. Where is Price?"

This man did know the crew or maybe he was one of them...long ago. "Captain Price is up there. *Capitán* Delgado seems to have a bone to pick with him, though."

"Captain?" the shaggy brows lifted again. "I daresay..." A smile shifted his beard.

Figuring this stringy haired prisoner had intimate knowledge of the *Sea Lion*'s crew, Angela asked, "Who are you?"

"Price," he said, holding out a filthy hand, "William Price."

Angela stared at the hand, dumbfounded. "But you're dead."

"Not yet, and I suddenly feel much livelier. What is your name, my lady?"

"Angela Foxe." Angela leaned over and took his hand, but William Price collected her fingers and tilted her wrist to kiss her knuckles. The formality of the time sent a tickle of appreciation through her.

"It's not every day I find a worthy pirate woman. Such a pleasure to meet you."

Angela couldn't help a grin at the intended compliment. "For what it's worth, I don't think we'll be alive much longer, and I don't know what to do about it. They're going to hang Captain Price and the rest of the crew they have up there. Delgado asked for nooses. I—I wanted to do something, anything, but they grabbed me, and I just...I wish I could do something."

Tears misted her eyes. If she'd done things differently, could she have prevented this? "I wanted to fight, to stop them all. But there's just so many, and I don't have any weapons. I asked them to show mercy. I pleaded with them, but they laughed. It's unfair what they're going to do to him, and I can't stop it." Emotion caught in her throat. Angela didn't realize just how far her caring went.

"I've seen men beg for their lives. I've heard their cries—far more often than I'd rather remember. The begging and pleading is always the same—spare me, save me, please don't do that. I can offer whatever in exchange... There's a difference with you. Your pleas ring true, but without concern over your own life. No, you and I are in the same situation, awaiting death or worse, but yet you worry for someone else." William paused and studied her.

Angela swiped tears from her eyes. It was true. She did care for Captain Price, and she wanted more than anything to save him.

"Do you love my brother?"

Love? Did she *love* Captain Price? Her instinct was to deny the accusation, but yet, she couldn't utter the denial. Love a man she'd only just met? The idea was ludicrous. And yet, when she pictured him and remembered his lips filling her body with tingles and need, and when he stood up for her, defended her, protected her... He was her hero, and all it earned him was a noose. Angela sobbed. The first man who'd treated her right was ripped from her grasp before they'd had a real chance. Why? What had she done wrong for the universe to throw her a curve ball? Angela struck out. She always sucked at sports. Angela composed herself and dashed away the tears with the dirt-streaked back of her hand.

The other prisoners rustled, now watching the evening's entertainment. Angela didn't care what they thought.

Since words failed her, William said, "Don't confuse me for a sap, but my brother is a good man. With my disappearance, I'm certain he's become...misdirected. He's always been devoted to the people in his life. As long as you're willing to give him your love, there's always hope."

His words were beautiful, but Angela couldn't find the hope behind thick iron bars, when an enemy captain had every intention of hanging Captain Price at any moment. For all she knew, he could already be dead. Angela's face twisted with her unrelenting tears.

William patted her shoulder in an attempt to console her while maintaining the respectful distance society demanded.

Screw society.

Angela fell into his arms, and he held her, gently patting her back and snagging his hands on her snarled hair.

"Oh, what is this?" William tugged on a tangle of strands.

"Leaves? Sand? Sticks?" For all she knew, Angela carried a family of chipmunks with her.

William tugged once more and freed something.

Angela leaned back and smiled. "It's a bobby pin. Supposed to hold my chaos in order. I think sticks would've worked better."

William inspected the small piece of metal and bent it. "Oh, no, sticks are far inferior compared to this. This... Do you know what this is?" Excitement once again lit his eyes.

Angela shook her head.

"My lady, this is hope. I think your wish is coming true. Do you have more of these?"

Angela sniffed and dug in her hair, dropping pin after pin on the floor.

"Take these to the others. We're getting out of here."

Angela scooped up her pins and roused each man who wasn't already enraptured with the drama in their cell and handed one to each. They accepted the pins and bent them like William did, and the prisoners quickly set to work on the locks holding their shackles closed. With Spain's numbers on deck, the *Sea Lion* crew had no chance, but with more men...

Angela remembered the captain's concern over the crew's numbers after the storm.

"If any of you are looking to join a pirate ship, the *Sea Lion* is hiring."

The tired men glanced at each other and mumbled. Some nodded.

William's shackles dropped free with a rattle of chains. He rubbed his wrists and ankles and stood, stretching his back and neck with a euphoric moan. "Far too long I've been stuck hunched over. A sweet kindness like none other. I'm in your debt, my lady Angela. How many soldiers are on deck?"

"Two dozen maybe. Enough."

More chains dropped, and the prisoners stood and approached the gate, but no one celebrated. They understood the gravity of what was to come. William worked at the tumbler standing between them and the warship full of soldiers.

"What's the plan?" Angela asked as William's tongue peeked between his lips.

The tumbler ticked and clicked until it thumped free. Prisoners gasped.

"Stay quiet. Overtake any man encountered and take his weapons. Make our way to the main deck. I need you all"—he nodded at the fellow prisoners—"to hold the soldiers on the main deck at gunpoint. I'm going after the captain."

"I'm going after Captain Price," Angela said. "Now let's get out of here."

William nodded with a smile, and he swung the iron gate open with an angry creak. One by one they filtered into the narrow gangway. The first soldier stood guard at the end of the hall, facing outward, as if more concerned about who was coming down rather than going up.

William covered the man's mouth to muffle an attempt at a warning shout and another prisoner behind him collected the knife at his belt. The prisoner stabbed the soldier, and softly he sunk to the floor.

As Angela passed him, the gurgles from his throat and drifting eyes made her queasy. The soldier was only doing his job, and he died for it. But if he didn't, none of them would survive the next twenty minutes.

Up the ladders they climbed through the decks, one after the other, on silent feet taking down oblivious soldiers and collecting a small arsenal to defend themselves with. Angela accepted a knife from William, hoping she didn't need to use it.

Chapter 24

AT THE FINAL LADDER to the main deck, William stopped to survey the scene, squinting into the daylight. His eyes weren't adjusted. How long had he been captive? Impatiently, Angela pushed her way up next to him. Four of the *Sea Lion*'s crew, including Buckley, stood on crates with nooses around their necks. The rest of the crew had soldiers holding them at gunpoint—at point-blank range.

Just away from the crew, Captain Price was buckled over on his knees with *Capitán* Delgado walking away from him and smirking. Price then fell over to the deck. Angela gasped. They were too late!

"Lift him up," *Capitán* Delgado said, sitting at a table...with tea? What the...? What kind of man could be so nonchalant about killing people? A monster. Delgado was a monster, who sipped from a teacup and said, "He must watch his men's deaths. On my count, remove the crates and let those feet swing free."

"No!" Angela whisper-yelled into William's ear. "Do something."

He hushed her. "We must coordinate our actions, or we are next."

William pointed at the prisoners waiting by his feet. "You fellows, go for the soldiers on the port side. Tell the men behind you to head starboard." The prisoners immediately conveyed the message while William turned to Angela. "Go for Price, but watch out for Delgado. He'll be desperate."

Angela gritted her teeth and gripped that knife. "He's never seen a woman scorned."

William's lips lazily lifted in a crooked smile. "Go!" he whispered, and they scrambled up the ladder, pouring through the narrow companionway. Angela booked across the deck with William at her side, heading straight for the one man who meant more to her than anything.

The soldiers paused and stared, dumbfounded with disbelief, and Angela and the prisoners used that to their advantage. She and William crossed the deck without any resistance, both carrying weapons at the ready and snarls on their faces.

Captain Price remained folded over.

Her insides swirled in fear of being too late.

The soldiers regained their wits and shouted, scrambling for defense. Swords were unsheathed. Guns were aimed and fired. Crew fell. Prisoners fell. The rapid pops around Angela shook her eardrums.

Prisoners reached the crew at the nooses and freed them, but not without consequences. Several prisoners dropped, and the freed crew took up their weapons. The surviving prisoners joined the crew in fighting back, but still they were far too outnumbered.

Angela turned away from the gruesome scene before she froze in panic and kept her legs moving across the deck. Perspiration dampened her already filthy clothing, and she startled when something or someone brushed against her foot, making her lose her balance, but Angela recovered and kept going. Through the chaos, Angela focused on Captain Price and tucking her knife into her rope belt. She didn't want to cut him accidentally.

Capitán Delgado's face pinched in fury at the sight of her. The gangly man launched to his feet, knife in hand. Right before the Delgado struck in rage, Angela ducked and William engaged the captain.

Angela slid to Captain Price. She held out her hands, wanting to touch him, but afraid of hurting him further, or of discovering she was too late.

"Captain Price?" she asked, voice shaky. "Captain Price, are you okay?"

A soft groan broke through his lips. Angela held her breath as her captain's head shifted. His shoulders tilted. Not believing her eyes, she brushed the hair out of his face.

Captain Price shuddered, and his face moved to meet her gaze. Surprise, worry, and relief flashed across his features. "Angela?"

Angela smiled. A flush of her own relief mixed with the heart-pounding adrenaline. Soon this would all be over, but whether they'd succeed was still up in the air. The sooner they got off this ship, the better their odds.

"I'm here."

"Call me Henry."

Angela smiled and inspected his hands for binds. "Henry, can you move?"

"I believe so." Henry's eyes lifted to Delgado, and they widened in fear. "Move!"

Angela looked up and ducked under a swinging blade, but it wasn't meant for her. William Price and Delgado were locked in a battle. Metal of meeting swords clanged in the air. The pistols, spent and too burdensome to reload, had been abandoned.

Buckley was ringed in uniformed bodies, but for an old fellow, he was shockingly skilled, holding back a handful of soldiers by himself. Angela's brows lifted. With him as an ally, she didn't need to worry about the others after all.

Cantu held his own also. A big lumbering giant, he had reach that the soldiers didn't.

A blade swooped through the air, and Angela rolled out of the way. Henry shuffled after her, folded with a hand pressed against his abdomen and a pinched face. Angela helped him to his feet, clear of the smaller skirmishes.

"Are you hurt?" she asked.

No longer the headstrong, determined man she'd met, now he was broken, in pain, lost. Henry pulled a bloody hand from his clothing.

"My need for vengeance clouded my judgment, but in all this time, I never truly believed I'd lose, and if I did, I was going to sacrifice myself to save those who bravely joined me." Henry lifted his eyes to the men fighting. Tears glistened on his lower lids. "I can't beat Delgado like this."

"We aren't trying to win. We're trying to survive. Escape. Get out of here while we still can."

"This is the end for me," Henry said, studying his bloody hand. "I've lived with many regrets in my life, but lately I've added so many more. I regret sailing into that storm, killing half my crew. I'd be sailing in depths with them if it weren't for you, my angel." Henry smiled, and his hand graced her jaw. "But I fear that effort was in vain. And I regret coming here, losing many more good men. Mostly I regret risking your life. I thought I lost you, and I was devastated."

Angela hated this goodbye speech. "Don't give up on me now. You have to live today and fight another day."

Henry shook his head. The defeat was crushing. "I won't give up my promise to you. Your safety is all that matters to me now, and I'm shocked you were able to escape, but somehow not surprised. You are strong, beautiful, and beyond anyone I deserve. I need you need to get out of here."

"We're both getting out of here now. All of us," Angela said. "I'm not that strong. It's only dumb luck that I escaped. You've been my protector all the while, and I need you. I need you to be strong, because you can't quit on me."

Henry's features twisted in surprise, looking over her shoulder, and before Angela reacted, Henry pushed her aside. Angela tumbled to the deck. There went her knee again. She flicked the nest of hair out of her face, and at the last second, Henry dodged an arcing blade from Delgado and William's fight.

Delgado disarmed William, who panted heavily. They were both bruised and bloodied, and their clothing torn. William had been in chains for so long, leaving him in this weakened state, how could he beat a healthier man?

Angela had to do something. The knife William had given her—Angela pulled it free from her belt and slid it across the deck. It stopped at William's bare foot. He bent and gripped it and rolled away from a strike.

Now she had no defense—not that she knew how to fight, anyway. More soldiers poured onto the deck from who knew where. They craned their necks, assessing the condition of their men. In moments, they would attack.

Henry rushed to her side and helped her to her feet. "Are you all right?"

"I will be when we're out of here. I need you, Henry. I need you to come with me. Your brother wouldn't want you to stay behind. Not like this." She spoke for the man, but she was certain she was right. She hoped her words got through to him, because they were almost out of time.

25

Chapter 25

ANGELA WANTED HIM SO dearly, could he choose to give up on her, too? It would break his heart to leave her when she needed him most. He'd already failed his brother, rest his soul, and now, wounded and bleeding, Price wouldn't fail Angela.

Besides, given the chance, his older brother would slap him upside the head for turning away from the chance at happiness right in front of him. He gripped Angela and held her close. With a confident smile on his face, "I won't quit on you. I shall not fail you. We must evacuate now."

Angry faces closed in and assessing them, Angela said, "Agreed."

"Abandon ship!" Henry roared and then winced at the ache in his gut. He really hated Delgado.

At the signal, the *Sea Lion* crew and the freed prisoners disengaged and rushed across the deck before throwing themselves over the rail. Delgado tracked one particular shaggy prisoner's retreat and roared, "This isn't over yet!"

The shaggy prisoner rushed to Angela, but Price didn't feel concerned over her safety. He had a feeling this man helped her escape. "We must go now. No delay!" The prisoner met Price's gaze for a flash as if to urge his escape, too.

Buckley and the others jumped from where they fought.

Only he and Angela remained, and the soldiers and vindictive captain closed the distance, holding swords aloft. No mercy remained on their bloodied faces.

Angela tugged on Henry's arm. "Can you swim?"

Henry had enough spirits in him to send her a small smile. "You first."

Angela nodded and climbed over the rail. Without hesitation, she jumped. He heard the splash and shifted to maneuver his legs over the rail. The enemy captain grabbed him by the shoulder, stopping him entirely.

"Henry! Captain Price!" she called from below, and the panic in her voice tore his heart.

She called again, "Henry!"

He couldn't answer. Calling back to her would only delay her escape, and there was nothing he could do from here. Price twisted free of Delgado's grip and stumbled over a downed man's outstretched arm. The victim was thin and woolly, wearing torn clothing. He appeared to be a prisoner. Freed from his burdens for only a minute to lose any hope forever. That could've been Price if Angela hadn't convinced him otherwise. A discarded body, waiting for disposal, never to be thought of again.

The grave injustice of Delgado's mere existence enraged Price, but the prisoner at his feet was barehanded.

"Mark my words," Delgado said in English, pointing a sword at Price's throat. "When the tide rolls a dawn tomorrow, the *Sea Lion* shall be volleyed into a cloud of smithereens, drifting quietly beneath the surface, and every last pirate on that wretched ship shall be hung under the gallows or making his peace with Davy Jones' Locker."

Price had learned his lesson, and thankfully, it appeared he wasn't too late after all…for Angela. Rather than engage the enemy he'd sworn to destroy, knowing it would be his useless end, Angela's words rolled through his mind, 'We aren't trying to win. We're trying to survive. You have to live today and fight another day'. As always, she was right. He could heal up, regroup, and do it right for the last time.

Without further hesitation, Price cast his enemy a smirk and flung himself overboard. *Please forgive me, dear brother.* He hit the water with a heavy splash and swam up. With far less clothing, the task was much easier, but Price was never a great swimmer. Gasping for air at the surface, he sought Angela, but he didn't see her. Price swiped his face clear.

"Angela?" he called and swam away from the ship. "Angela!"

"Henry!"

Captain Price exhaled in relief at her voice. A lightness filled him as he paddled toward her. She'd been halfway to shore, but she turned around for him.

"Stay there. I'll come to you."

She didn't listen.

Price paddled harder, so she didn't return within range of the *Peibo del ler San Francisco*, and he caught up to her a safe distance from the enemy warship.

"Are you okay?" she asked, brow creased in worry.

"I'll be fine." But his abdominal wound now leaked rapidly in the water.

"There's something I need to tell you," Angela said.

"It can wait. Let's get out of the water." Price paddled toward shore, keeping a close eye on Angela to be sure she stayed at his side. He'd never expected to survive that ship a second time. He'd lost men, again, but at least he didn't have to lose someone he loved.

Last time it was William.

This time it would've been Angela.

He'd been spared that pain, and for that, he was eternally grateful. He touched sand and stood. Angela panted, marching out of the water. He held his hand out to her, and she took it. He assisted her through the soft sand underfoot.

They both needed a break, but Spain would destroy the *Sea Lion*, and Price couldn't let that happen. "We must return to the ship immediately."

Angela wiped water from her face. "Why?"

A flicker of movement caught Price's attention. A man revealed himself from the jungle, and Price turned, shoving Angela behind him. The filthy but soaked man was one of the prisoners. The one who'd fought *Capitán* Delgado.

"State your name, sir," Price called over.

Angela pushed around Price, refusing his protection. "He won't hurt me."

After all they'd survived, Price couldn't take that risk. "How do you know such things? Look at his condition. He was clearly a prisoner. What do you think he did to earn that spot?"

"What did I do?" Angela retorted.

She had a point. Price waited for the stranger to approach and speak. His clothing draped on his thin frame like rags. His disheveled hair and overgrown beard obscured his features, but despite all that, he walked with a familiar confidence. The gleam in his eye reminded him of...

Angela stepped back to give them space. A small smile lifted her lips.

It couldn't be. Could it? After all this time and complete certainty of the man's fate, was it possible? No, no, it couldn't be. The Spaniards—Delgado and his father—held the man surrounded by swords. Death had been imminent. Price had seen it with his own eyes! Delgado had claimed they made a deal—William had publicly admitted his crimes of piracy, turned himself over, and was hung for it. But Price had never heard the story. The pirate reputation had never been tarnished. There was no reasonable chance the man strolling across the sand was his William, but still his heart wanted to believe.

"Brother?" Price asked with a whisper.

"It's I, brother." William pulled Price into a hug.

Tears pricked his tired eyes. A crazed laugh rose from within, and Price burst in laughter, in relief, in true amazement. His chest swelled with appreciation and relief. They patted each other's backs and squeezed. Price never wanted to let go.

"I thought I'd lost you." A sob broke through his celebratory laughter.

William shifted back from his embrace. "The Spaniards busied themselves with other matters, so I was stashed away for future use. They never expected you to arrive and throw them into disarray. And they never expected a woman to set us free."

William gestured Angela to come closer. The beautiful woman had tears of joy in her eyes, and when she stepped forward, Price and his brother pulled her into a tight squeeze.

"I owe you my life in so many ways," Price told her. "I am forever in your debt."

"That's not necessary. I didn't do it for accolades," Angela said.

"Then why did you risk your life for me and William?"

Price and William loosened their grip on her. She sniffled and leaned back to look him in the eyes. "Because I love you."

The world around them dropped away. All Price saw was her. The kind soul who risked everything for him; she showed him real life—one free of a pact to destroy an enemy nation—was possible. A blossom of heat rose through his chest, unlocking tingles of need and desire he hadn't felt in so long. Being so near his brother, he shoved those feelings down for later.

But the buzz trembling through his brain was real, and he knew just what to say, "My dearest Angela, I've loved none other but you, and it's because of you that I breathe. You are an angel, and I shall cherish the ground you traverse for all of my days."

"I've never heard such sentiment from you, brother," William said with a chuckle. "I'm thrilled that heart of yours is capable of it, but Spain is sure to send soldiers ashore after us, and I'd hate for our little reunion to be dashed so soon. Let us set sail at once."

Price, now realizing William witnessed his whole declaration of love, blushed furiously, but his brother was right. And they had bigger problems than soldiers chasing them. "Delgado claimed he shall volley the *Sea Lion* at high tide. We must go now."

"Are you certain?" William asked.

"Delgado follows through on his threats. After we escaped his clutches twice, he won't stop until we're dead—orders from the Crown or not."

"Then we hurry. Where does she anchor?"

Price pointed to the entrance of the cove. "Southeast by south, around the cove entrance."

More filthy men appeared from the jungle, and Price turned on them in defense. After getting a miraculous second chance with the people he loved most, he'd never allow anyone to harm Angela or his brother.

William touched his shoulder in reassurance. "These are good men."

"I invited them," Angela said. "I thought after the wreck you were shorthanded. They can sail."

Price stared at her in surprise. "You invited them? Where did you find these filthy men?"

"The warship's prisoners. Most of them are English merchant sailors."

Just when he thought he'd seen all her surprises, Angela pulled yet another out of a labyrinthine bag. Price turned to the shy crowd, beaming with hope. "All who want to join the *Sea Lion*, follow us for a fair share and freedom. You are most welcome."

William led the way, and Price collected Angela's hand. They marched just inside the jungle, out of direct line of sight of the Spaniards, and a line of men followed behind. No matter the struggles before them, Price had never been happier.

Chapter 26

ANGELA CRUNCHED TWIGS AND short plants under her steps and ducked under low-hanging branches. She was exhausted and overdue for sleep, and her salty, damp clothing irritating, but Angela walked on soft clouds. A lightness lifted her, giving her the energy to float through the dense jungle behind William. Henry insisted on staying behind her to keep an eye on both her and his brother. Personally, she'd rather have Henry's round ass to marvel at while they walked, but considering what Henry went through, she humored his minor request.

Angela yawned.

"You best be staying awake there," a familiar voice said. Buckley popped out of the woods and joined them. Cantu was just behind them.

"Price," Buckley addressed one of the men. "And Price," he addressed the other.

The brothers both gestured their welcome. They were both tired, too.

Henry said, "You made it, Buck. Cantu, good to see you."

Cantu nodded.

"I didn't think we were going to survive," Buckley said. "But I'm glad I'm not a betting man. You did good back there, for a woman." Buckley fell in stride alongside her.

"Uh, thanks." Angela didn't have the energy to correct Buckley's quip, not that she alone could change his mind, so she accepted his compliment as he meant it.

"Is Delgado finally dead?" Buckley asked.

Henry spoke up, a harshness in his voice. "He lives."

Buckley's brows rose. "All that plotting, planning, and stewing, and you let him get away?"

Henry darted him a look of annoyance. "I know when I'm outmatched, and since I have what I wanted, I have no reason to further my campaign against him."

"Huh. Something sure has changed with you, and I don't think the elder Price was the reason," Buckley added and glanced at Angela.

At Henry's silence, Angela looked at him. She smiled, and he winked in return. With the top few buttons of his tunic torn off, the peeking chest hair sent tingles crawling down her aching body. What else lay beneath that fabric precariously clinging to his skin? More jewelry like his glinting ear? She wanted to peel it off and find out.

Tongues optional.

Waiting for a private moment for just the two of them left her heart thumping and her mind a swirling mess. She hadn't been with any man since Brandon, and those were memories she'd rather delete. Instead, she shifted her gaze to Henry, wishing to strip every layer of fabric off his body and explore every inch of skin. He was a beautiful man, and he'd do anything to keep her safe.

She'd never felt more important in her life.

Henry had been adamant about returning her home, but with her admission, would he change his mind? Angela wasn't certain on much, but she knew life aboard a ship wasn't for her. Would Henry's call for the sea keep him from her? Did he mean to keep his promise: *safe passage to whatever destination you choose?* He'd known she was from the future. She still never got a chance to ask how he knew that.

A branch struck her in the face.

"Ow!" Angela flinched and cradled her cheek. A greater force was sending her a message, but she had no idea what it meant.

"Are you injured?" Henry asked.

"It's just a scratch." Angela turned to show him, and the sight of blood on his tunic made her gasp. She stopped in her tracks. When she'd seen Henry curled up on the deck and the captain walking away, she'd assumed Delgado punched him in the abdomen or kicked him in a sensitive region. "What is that? Is that what Delgado did?"

Henry gestured at it and waved it off. "It's nothing. Do not worry yourself over me."

William stopped his lead and returned to them. "We're almost out of the cove. What's the commotion back here? Oh." William lifted the sticky shirt from Henry's abdomen and checked the wound over. "How deep did it go?"

"Five centimeters, give or take. It's nothing. We must reach the *Sea Lion* and set sail before the tide returns."

William frowned at it. "Does the vessel have a medic on board?"

"Meeks was struck down by a Royal Navy man-o'-war, and his replacement retired inland."

"So, that means no. Buckley?"

"I can fix the ship with my tools. I don't see much resemblance between a wooden beauty and"—Buckley eyed the captain pointedly—"a flesh and blood man, but I'll do my best."

"Buckley, your hands tremble like palm trees in a squall," Henry countered.

Like Henry's hesitation, Angela liked the old man, but not enough to allow him to fix the captain's wound. "I can do it, if you have supplies for me to work with."

"Excellent," William said. "Let's get to it."

"Riley would know if the doctor's chest survived the sinking." Henry collected Angela's hand and smiled in reassurance. It didn't work. If his brother was that concerned, she was doubly so. Her stomach knotted as he led her out of the safety of the jungle and down the beach, out of the cove.

The tide had crept in, and the *Sea Lion* was afloat. They'd left a longboat just in case, and the survivors and escapees climbed inside and rowed as the sunrise blinded them. After being locked in that eye-watering cell, the sea breeze was a welcomed fresh air.

Henry and William urged her up the hull first, and the brothers climbed up behind her. She felt special. She felt loved and protected. And she smiled as she clambered over the rail. Buckley and the other established crew, who'd survived, followed closely. The prisoners stayed behind in the longboat.

Moving over the rail, Henry winced, holding his abdomen. That was her priority.

"Riley!" Henry shouted.

The quartermaster popped out of the navigation room at once and approached while assessing their condition. "You made it out. Sort of. I guess that means I'm not the captain.

Thankfully, I'm glad you're back." Riley smiled, but Henry didn't share his relief. "What happened?"

"Did Vallo return?" Henry asked.

"No. What's this about?"

"No time to explain. Is she sea ready?" Henry asked.

"I'm afraid not. All the holes have been patched in the hull to the best our supplies allowed, and I believe with fair weather, she'll make it to a safer port, but the rigging is still a mess. Karl said we need weeks to sort the tangled lines. Without them, we're at the sea's mercy."

"There's no way to move this ship before dusk?" Henry asked again.

"Not in our current position, captain. Maybe if we had more men." Riley scanned the deck, worry settling on his features. "No others survived? The few of you, that's all?"

"Not exactly," Angela said, and Riley sent her a confused glance.

"Bring up the new recruits," Henry told his brother.

Riley scrutinized their small group more closely. "New recruits? What happened? Who's that?" He nodded toward William.

William gestured over the rail for the prisoners to come aboard and moved aside. "We need hands. They need a vessel."

"Well," Riley said with a smile. "This is great! Who are you?"

William approached Riley. "William Price, former Royal Navy armorer, former *Sea Lion* armorer, and former *Peibo del ler San Francisco* prisoner."

Riley grinned. "Captain Price's brother has risen from the grave."

"Feels that way," William said, rubbing the nape of his neck.

The prisoners filtered onto the deck, and Riley greeted them. "Hope has been restored."

"Riley," Henry said, "You can thank Angela." Henry winked at her.

Heat of appreciation warmed her. Angela ached to scurry him to his cabin and inspect his wound. Inspect other things. She wanted to capture his lips, strip him naked, show her appreciation for a long, long time. She'd never wanted a man more than Henry at this very minute and the throbbing down below wouldn't let up.

The quartermaster approached her, wearing the features of a conflicted man. Angela swallowed. Lust fully extinguished. She'd forgotten for just a moment how much she wasn't welcome on this ship. "I owe you an apology. Woman or not, you have proved yourself worthy of a place on the *Sea Lion*. If any of the crew continues hostilities against you, send for me at once. Because of you, we have a chance to escape this enemy island. Thank you."

"You're welcome." Angela smiled.

Pirates or not, these were good men—well, mostly. Angela squeezed the edge of her tunic, wringing out excess water. Drops pattered to the wood floor, reminding her of Henry's wet wound. "Did the doctor's chest survive the wreck? We need it."

"Who's injured?" Riley asked.

"Price has a knife wound. It needs tending before all these efforts to destroy Delgado end with gangrene," William said.

"Buckley," Riley said, and the carpenter disengaged from the newcomers. "You remember where the chest is?"

"If they put it back where they found it, then I do."

"Will you assist Angela and Price below deck?" Riley asked.

"Consider it done. Come with me, you two," Buckley said.

"Which Price?" William asked with a naughty smirk.

Henry slapped his brother upside the back of the head playfully. "She's mine, and don't you ever forget it."

William chuckled and rubbed his head. "Feathery gull."

Angela didn't know what that meant, but she figured it was a friendly insult between brothers. She followed Buckley while holding Henry's hand, and on their way across the deck, several of the prisoners patted her on the back in thanks. A shiver of excitement filled her as she climbed down the ladder to find the medical supplies. She was respected, accepted.

Once the darkness enveloped her, that excitement waned. She needed to save Henry's life.

Again.

27

Chapter 27

HOLDING HENRY'S HAND AND trying to ignore the current his touch zipped through her, Angela stopped on the ladder before plowing into Buckley. He paused, and she squinted into the dim interior to see what the matter was. Shimmers of light...on the floor? She squinted harder.

"The bilge pumps ain't keeping up, but now that we have men, shouldn't be a problem." Buckley jumped off the ladder and landed knee deep in water. "The infirmary is back here. The chest maybe wet, but it was put back after the wreck."

Angela sighed before getting wet again, and Henry entered the water without hesitation. Thankfully, his wound stayed out of the water this time. Her tired legs fought the water tension, and she brushed aside floating debris.

Through the mess hall with wooden bowls floating in the corner, Buckley stopped inside a narrow doorway and swung his arm wide. "Here it is. Good luck. Hope you sew up well, captain."

Buckley left to return to work—or maybe catch some sleep.

Angela scanned the tight room half-filled with water. "Is there any light around here?"

"Even if I found a lantern, I have nothing dry to light a candle with," Henry said, releasing her hand and sitting on a barrel.

Angela groaned in frustration and struck out her hands, approaching a shelf. She knocked over something metal and left it. Round objects, conical objects, a small crate. A book! She handed that to Henry. "Hold on to this."

Her fingers kept searching blindly until she found a handle connected to a large box, but it was out of reach. "Can you help get this off the shelf?" She hated to ask, but if it was what she needed, then getting it was better than not.

Henry sloshed over. "Is there anything else down here you wish to use?"

"I don't know what most of this stuff is."

"I don't suppose a woman from the future would," Henry said gently.

At confirmation she hadn't heard him wrong before, Angela turned. Eyes adjusted, his features were outlined in a soft light. "How did you know? How could you possibly...?" She mumbled, brain misfiring. Too many questions and not enough time.

"Angela, you aren't the first."

Angela blinked several times while processing that statement. People regularly traveled to the past? Was it some government technology they kept secret? How could someone hundreds of years into the past understand a phenomenon known only as science fiction in the future? If others had been here before her, then there is a way home.

Angela reached again to help Price lower it off the shelf, and the old vendor's amethyst necklace in her pocket pressed against her thigh. Her smile waned. Since the moment she'd arrived, she'd been asking herself how she was going to get home. The act of placing it over her head brought her here. The act of taking it off had no effect. So Angela could only assume placing it back over her head would bring her home. But now with Henry's sweet smile fluttering through her like a bunch of drunk butterflies, obscuring her thoughts, testing that theory no longer seemed so important.

Price collected the chest off the shelf. "Let us get out of the water. You'll catch a chill."

"Right." Angela frowned and quickly searched the shelf, indecipherable objects puzzling her worn brain. "I don't think there's anything else useful, but I'm flying blind here."

Henry made an amused noise.

"I...I mean—"

"The concept of flying is intriguing, but I can surmise your meaning. Come then. We must be on our way. There's much to be done."

Angela pushed her way through the rising water and followed Henry, who shouldered the burden of the chest himself.

Guilt weighed on her. "Let me help you with that."

"A lady doesn't assist in a man's duty."

The brush off sparked frustration. "I don't care if you think you don't need help, give me a side before you make that injury worse."

Henry paused, but didn't relent.

"This stubborn pride of yours is going to lead to surgery, and there's no doctor out here. Unless you want Buckley rooting around your insides, let me help carry."

Henry sighed. "It's a habit I'm afraid shall take much time to break. Forgive me, but if anyone asks about your assistance, inform them that my wound is much worse than it is, especially William."

Angela snorted. "Didn't you hear Riley? He thanked me. I'm no longer a useless, cursed woman on their ship. They aren't going to think less of you for needing my help. And if any of them secretly thinks so, well, they can go fu—" Angela stopped abruptly. Getting Henry to see her side was one thing. With a ship full of men who'd just welcomed her, equality wasn't an argument worth bringing up right now.

"They can what?" Henry asked, amusement lurking on his lips.

Angela gripped a handle alongside his fingers and headed up the ladder first. "Never mind."

Henry stood firm, and the chest jerked in her hand. "I insist you tell me what you planned to say. No need to hide your curious thoughts on the matter."

"You really want to know?"

"I insist."

"I was going to say that where I'm from women are just as capable as men. We're not dainty flowers who need chaperones. I drive a forklift and carry heavy shipments of merchandise every day for work, just like my male peers. I can handle this chest, and I can handle a few sassy men. I'll admit, if they all came after me, they'd win, but if the situation were reversed—a bunch of women after one man, he'd lose, too. It's beyond frustrating to me to be treated like I'm less than. My skills make me no better or worse than any of this crew, if I were given the chance to learn how to sail."

"I agree with you—" Henry started.

Angela's frustrated speech continued, not registering his words. "And for that matter, I helped patch the hole below deck, and I can swing a hammer just as well as anyone. I can hit a nail better than Buckley. But it's a good thing we have Giles, because if you wanted the lady on the ship to cook..." Angela laughed. "We'd starve."

Henry reached out and touched her hand. "I said I agree with you."

"Then why are you being stubborn about carrying the chest?"

"Do you have its weight?"

Angela tilted her chin up. "I couldn't reach it, but I can carry it."

"You are not equal to the men on this ship." He paused and fury boiled within her. "You're better. But not all of them know you the way I do, and I need to maintain the appearance of strength even in the face of injury. The sooner I can be at my best, the sooner we can get out of here. I fear vulnerability in the eyes of the company."

Henry slowly released the handle she'd been holding, and Angela caught it. The chest was heavy, but no big deal.

Angela's heart softened for him. "I understand the important of keeping up appearances. Truly, I do. So long as we're in this together, I won't let anyone hurt you."

The captain snorted. "I should be the one professing my protection to you. Instead, I find myself desiring the touch of your lips."

Heat rushed through Angela's body, sparking energy she'd thought was all spent, quickly renewing her need to touch him. "Then kiss me."

"It's a risk with the crew nearby, and their favor of you is finally tilting in the right direction."

Angela released the chest on a half-submerged barrel. "Shut up and kiss me."

With desperation in his eyes, Henry closed the distance. Angela flung her arms around him, and her lips met his. The kiss wasn't satisfying. It only made her crave more. She wanted all of him. Angela shifted her lips against his smooth but wanting kiss, her hands clawing at his back, urging him closer. The pivotal fear popped back into her head, and tears wet her eyelids. Would he survive the injury? And if he did, could she leave him? Angela pulled away and brushed the tears aside.

"That's not the reaction I usually get." Henry's dark blue eyes filled with concern.

Angela couldn't hold his gaze. "Let's get you patched up."

"Are you all right?"

She was. He wasn't. Angela nodded and lifted the chest. She climbed the stairs, glancing over her shoulder for the captain's ascent. She watched his flinches with each of his steps, and worry settled on her shoulders.

THE CREW HAD BEEN too busy working on the ship's repairs to notice her and Henry on their way to his private chambers, or they didn't care. She'd dreaded returning to the room that almost drowned her and was responsible for the quartermaster's assumptions turning the crew against her. But as Henry sat on the now-dry mattress, and Angela opened the chest at the foot of the bed, suddenly the soft bedding and peace and quiet were very appealing. She was so tired her eyeballs hurt. Yep, that was a thing.

Henry lifted his tunic, and Angela took a beat to marvel at him. A pair of gold rings hung from his nipples and scars crisscrossed his rounded pecs. He was beautiful, experienced, hardened. She dragged her eyes to his wounds and inspected them with bated breath. Would he be okay? Judging by the condition of it, she assumed the stab had been a clean cut with no organ damage, but every time he shifted, the wound's edges popped apart. "Lift higher. Since I have you here, I want to see that slice from Berger."

Henry did. The sword gash was scabbed over and dirty. "There's nothing I can do for that. It should heal fine." She hated to see him in pain, much less be the cause of it, but Delgado's stab needed closing to heal. The daylight from the row of windows at the stern was enough to work with, but she needed something to sterilize the needle.

"Lie down for me please." Angela rifled through the chest and lit a candle. Speaking softly, she asked, "How did you know I'm from the future? Is it common around here?"

"I met another like you, but no, it's not common at all. I recommend you don't tell another where you came from."

Angela thoroughly heated the needle, and when she turned, the captain had removed his tunic entirely. His head rested on his arm as a pillow. Angela reached over, grabbed his actual pillow, and swapped them out for his comfort. He smiled. "Thank you."

"Hang on tight. This is going to hurt." Taking a deep breath, she poked his flesh.

Henry winced and pressed his lips thin as Angela tugged the line through. "What did you mean by another like me?"

The captain exhaled slowly. "Our previous captain, Lemoine, entrusted information to me that I believed to be the words of a madman. I'd feared for his well-being and insisted he sought help. I was not as gentle as I should've been. He was our leader, voted to be the best of us, and my concerns for his mental clarity in his position were valid. I urged him to keep his foolish ideas to himself and never speak of them again."

"What did he say?"

"Lemoine insisted our newest crewman was from the future. He'd claimed to have seen proof, but he could not share with me. I never believed his tale until I saw you. I checked the hold myself only minutes prior to your appearance. No man on the *Sea Lion* saw you either, at port nor after. Since you're not a mermaid, the only explanation is Lemoine told the truth. Imagine my relief in learning my best friend had not lost his mind. Is there such a device in the future which allows travel through time? I can only imagine the possibilities."

"Time travel is science fiction where I'm from. Well..." Angela trailed off. "It *was*. Now I'm not sure of anything anymore. Hold still." She inserted the needle one last time and knotted off the ends. The bleeding stopped. "That's the best I can do."

Henry inspected his fine, flat abdomen dusted with a sexy layer of dark hair. He was a gorgeous man and Angela almost sighed at the sight. Henry yawned and tried to sit up. "I thank you kindly for your services. I'd rather stay here with you, but I must return to work. You can guard the supplies or come with me. I believe my crew shall treat you well."

Angela stopped him with a hand on his firm chest. He hardly resisted; a feather could've pushed him back. "No. As your doctor, I am ordering you to sleep. The men can work during the day, and you and I are getting rest. If you want to successfully evade Spain before dawn, we need to sleep."

"Under one condition." Henry's blinks slowed, eyelids heavy with the need for sleep and healing, and Angela yawned.

"What's that?"

"Join me."

She wanted to so damned desperately. "Is that a good idea? It didn't go well last time we were caught together."

"Much has changed since then."

Angela smiled and closed up the medicine chest. Henry splayed on the mattress, and Angela tucked alongside him, warm and comfortable. His chest rose and fell with soft even breaths within moments. Angela drifted off seconds later.

Chapter 28

FOR THE FIRST TIME since she'd arrived in the past, Angela woke without worrying about the state of her mental health. Her eyes fluttered open, and a grin pulled at her lips. Henry was still snoozing next to her. He hadn't moved the whole day. Night shrouded the cabin in darkness. Such an eerie feeling to have no source of light but the moon. Cities bled light into the skies. Satellites and airplanes showed signs of life moving around. Not here. Just a splinter of moonlight reflecting off the gentle waves of the sea.

Angela yawned and sat up to stretch. Henry shifted next to her. His hand moved to where she'd laid, and his eyes popped open at once. "Angela?"

"I'm right here." She took his hand. "How are you feeling?"

"Better. I needed that rest." His head swiveled toward the windows.

"I don't sense any movement. Are we still anchored off Cuba?"

Angela laughed. "I forget to get a status update before you woke. Let's go find out."

"Right, right." Henry stood and together they left the cabin. The men were still working hard at repairs, exhaustion slowed their movements. Giles walked around handing out plates to the men where they stood, skipping dining in the mess all together. Angela caught a plate for her and Henry, who had bigger concerns at the moment.

"Riley!" Henry shouted.

The quartermaster turned from Karl and approached with a smile. "Glad to see you on your feet."

"Why haven't we set sail yet?" Henry asked with increasing urgency.

"Karl just informed me the *Sea Lion* should be in ship shape by tomorrow mid-afternoon."

"You're certain?"

"You can ask him yourself." Riley pointed to where Karl directed the prisoners. The newcomers pulled lines and others untangled them. Crew wove lines around cleats, knotting them taut. A smooth oiled machine, they worked well and efficiently. But from the sound of it, not efficient enough. Angela released her captain's hand and helped herself to the pork.

Henry rubbed his face from forehead to chin. "Never thought I'd say the words, but we must abandon ship."

Riley snorted. "Abandon ship? Are you mad? We're stranded on Spain's territory and loaded with treasure. If we don't get out of here soon, Delgado is bound to find us."

"It's too late," Henry said on an exhale as if defeated. "*Capitán* Delgado and the Spanish warship *Peibo del ler San Francisco* are just around the corner. He vowed to volley this ship when the tide permits them to maneuver into range at dawn. We won't escape."

"You're certain?" Paleness hollowed Riley's features.

"Completely," Henry said. "Load up the longboats with anything of value on board. We're taking a new ship."

Riley shook his head. "If you think we can take a Spanish warship as prize, you, dear sir, have lost your mind. I will not agree to it, and nor will they."

"We are taking the English schooner they captured. Only a half dozen or so Spaniard soldiers are guarding it. After all, who would be foolish enough to attempt such a thing with the warship anchored right next to it?" Price grinned deviously. "With our newest recruits and their dwindled numbers, overwhelming the schooner shall be easy, and when Spain appears around that headland at dawn, they shall be sorely disappointed to find us on the horizon, instead, sailing their prize."

Riley groaned. "I cannot argue your logic. I'll relay the message to the crew." The quartermaster turned and shouted, "Eat up and unload this ship!"

Angela stifled a laugh at the unexpectedly impromptu orders.

Before the quartermaster could run off, giving more orders, Henry recaptured his attention. And the excitement fell from the younger man's face. "Tell me you don't have more bad news."

"Only a question. We spent the day together in my cabin. Why didn't you accuse Angela and I of breaking the articles?"

"I trust you," Riley said. "Besides, the ship wasn't rocking, so I didn't bother knocking."

Angela's face heated. She'd needed the rest, but if Henry was capable of that, she wanted him. She wanted all of it.

Henry's brows lifted and his cheeks flushed. It was cute. "Why, thank you for assuming I have such prowess in bed."

Angela laughed. Riley grinned and patted him on the shoulder. "Don't let the words swell your skull!" Riley rushed off to coordinate the crew's efforts.

With a smile, Henry held out his hand as if expected her to accept it, but Angela handed him his plate.

"That's not what I wanted, but on second thought, my stomach is empty."

"I remember scraping by from one meal to the next, and I can't say I ever liked it."

"We try to avoid it. Keeps the crew content to have a belly full. If we can manage tonight, I don't think anyone will worry about their next meal." Price finished his plate, took her empty, and added them to Giles's stack. He brushed his fingers clean and asked, "Now where were we?"

"I don't know," Angela said, confused.

The devious grin returned, and Price gestured for her to follow him back into the cabin. Sparks of heat roared through her, picturing exactly what she wanted to do, but with his injury, she'd never attempt it. Perhaps there was something else they could to in the meantime...

Henry lifted the medicine chest.

Angela rushed over and took the weight of it. "Do you want to rip stitches? Because that's how you rip stitches."

"We all must do our best."

"Your best is leading, not lifting. Let go."

While deadlocked in a staring contest for power, William Price entered the cabin, holding his plate and chewing. "You two are quite the entertainment. Best listen to the lady, dear brother. You've made it this far. We'd hate to lose you to a petty cut from Delgado."

Henry broke eye contact to glare at his brother. "I'll be fine."

"Says every man ever injured and trying to do something stupid," Angela countered.

The brothers stared each other down.

"Don't be so stubborn. Angela can help the crew by lifting the precious cargo. You can help by leading this desperate folly. Unless...you'd prefer me to take over as captain."

Henry released the chest and asked, "Do you want to?"

Talking with his mouth full, William pointed his meaty rib at his own chest. "Me? Oh, brother, no. I'm not taking the blame for this. Even if you get us away from this island in one piece and the crew wished it, no."

Henry's lips thinned. "Dreams change?"

William chewed and cast Angela a knowing look. "Indeed." The captain's brother strolled out.

"What was that about?" Angela asked, holding the chest.

Henry raked a hand through his dark locks. "We were supposed to sail together as captains. Create our own flotilla, doubling our prowess on the seas under the black. But after his *presumed* death, it could never happen. I hated the sea, and I never wanted to step foot in saltwater again. As he confirmed, dreams change."

"I'm sorry things didn't turn out how you wanted." Angela's pork settled heavily. Price wanted to stay on the sea. His old dream had returned with his brother, but they wouldn't sail their own ships. Perhaps share one. Knowing she and Price wanted different things was hard to swallow, and the weight of the necklace in her pocket suddenly got much heavier.

Chapter 29

With their supplies safely on shore, a handful of oil lamps lit their meager supplies. "Load the vanguard with the best pistols and sharpest swords. We're going after the English schooner now. The rest of you stay on shore to guard the supplies and treasure. I don't suspect you'll be harassed, but be prepared." After they'd escaped from Delgado's ship, they'd added more men to their crew, but also pistols. It still wasn't enough for everyone.

Captain Price needed Angela, not because of her brilliant language skills, but because he loved her. This woman, who simply glowed in the soft light, marveling at the weapons before her, saved his life more than he could count. And now she was by his side, ready to save the crew. Captain Price wouldn't leave her behind with the crew in charge of the supplies. Not with Vallo out there somewhere. Not with Spain lurking. He didn't trust any of his crew to defend her as much as him.

Maybe Buckley, Cantu, and Riley. But he needed their skills on the vanguard.

Maybe William.

...eh, probably not.

Price selected a pair of pistols, one cutlass, and two daggers. He added a third at his ankle, checking each for integrity prior to equipping them.

Angela lifted a hammer. "I'll take this."

"Excellent choice," Henry said. "but take this, too." He held out a small dagger. "Strap it to your ankle like mine."

She stared at his open palm. "Is it necessary? I'm more comfortable with the hammer."

"It's better to have and not need then the other way around."

"Okay."

Figuring the foreign term to originate in the future, he determined it meant both acquiescence and a favorable state of being. The future sounded confusing. But the women, judging by the two he'd met, were far more open about their stances and opinions. They refused to bow to the rule of men, and they made themselves known. Something about that forwardness made Price visualize a woman in bed with a strong knowledge of what she wanted and how she wanted it. Remembering her warm lips grazing his sensitive skin sent a heat of desire roaring through his loins. He desperately wanted to test his hunch.

If he survived the night, of course.

With each what *if* and *but*, the odds of survival dwindled dramatically. He saw no other outcome but taking the schooner, and he'd do everything to secure Angela's safety, for he knew of someone she'd want to see.

Angela strapped the blade to her ankle, and Price focused on her backside, bending in his face. Just beyond her luscious shape, the shifting of his brother caught his eye.

No matter how much his brother had endured, William needed to prepare, too. "Wait here. I'll return swiftly."

Angela nodded, and Price filled his hands with extra weapons. While the vanguard armed themselves by the light, William was busy relieving himself against a palm tree.

"Take these," Price insisted.

William, still holding himself, said, "My hands are busy. Care to wait?"

"At the rate of your watering, Spain will find us standing here and kill us all."

"Such a dramatist. You, my dearest brother, should write down your tales of embellishment. I care to absorb such words while emptying my bowels at the head."

Price held the weapons closer. "We have no time for games. I've spent ages waiting to hunt your killer only to discover not only were you alive, but apparently well enough to retain your sense of humor."

William shook himself clear of drips and a seriousness eliminated the jesting. "I regret the loss of your freedom of mind. I knew once Spain had accepted my offer, they'd deliver me wholly to the authorities for a spectacle at the gallows, and you'd waste the rest of your life avenging me. In my cell, wondering why the journey had been taking so long, I thought of nothing else except you biding your time for the right moment to pursue the enemy. Focusing on Delgado would've driven you mad with obsession. I regret what he's done to you. At the time, I could see no other way, but this isn't you. This wasn't us."

On the verge of battle, Price couldn't lose himself to emotions tearing him apart. Calmly, he said, "Take them. I cannot bear the thought of you being killed or recaptured. Take these, for my sake."

"You remember why we took to the seas?" William accepted the extra weapons and tucked them appropriately on his person. "We had nothing left for us back home, so we joined the Royal Navy together to fight Spain, but we endured punishment unfit for a dog. We gladly accepted the offer of freedom by Wilcox. Remember our first captain? Do you remember what he wanted?"

Price just stared. He knew, but he didn't want to say it.

"Wilcox wanted love, but to have it, he needed the money to be worthy. So he took the money he needed."

A story told a thousand times. "Certainly, but Wilcox was last seen at The Golden Macaw, stumbling around drunk. Lot of good it did him."

"I believe you. I also believe his gambling addiction bested him. But that is not my point here, brother. He wasted his life trying to get something, and he lost it. Then he wasted the rest of his life miserable. My point is you have that lovely lady over there. She's the reason why I'm here with you. Don't let her get away and don't let your obsession with vengeance destroy your future. That's over."

Frustrated with his brother's lack of understanding over the situation, Price said, "It's not me who keeps us apart. It's her need to return home." Price glanced over his shoulder at the woman glowing by the flickering light, seated on a log, inspecting the hammer she'd chosen. Why would an amazing woman like her want to give up everything for him? "It's my doubt—"

William uttered a dismissive grunt. "Then change her mind! Dear God, Henry, your head is a bag of cats. You're a predator on the water. You take what you want for sport. Do you want her? Then take her!"

Price sighed. His brother didn't understand. Some days he wished for that careless, worry-free sentiment. But Captain Price knew what was right there, but he wouldn't take her. He respected her too much to force her into something she didn't want. She had to choose him and his world.

"Thank you for the words of wisdom, as always," Price said with a hint of mockery, because William wasn't known for making wise choices. And his advice was terrible. Price returned to Angela's side.

She smiled sweetly at him. Would she give up her home for him? Would she consider staying for *him*? Would Price be as lucky as Lemoine? None of these questions mattered a lick if their attempt tonight ended unsuccessfully, but knowing the answer would propel him further toward success.

Price smiled back. "I must ask you something of great consequence. The answer is a difficult one, but I must know before our excursion for my own selfish reasons. Could you bear the question for me?"

Her face tilted with endearing confusion. "You can ask me whatever you want, and I'll do my best to give you an answer. Is that what you're asking?"

Price collected both her hands in his. Ignoring the crew's curious eyes, he asked her softly, "Will you consider, if we survive the night, which the outcome is not certain... Now, just for a moment, if you will, could you see the possibility of a home here, but not here, somewhere else, wherever you want. In essence... I'm... I'm failing to articulate my thoughts properly."

"You want me to do something. The rest is not so clear." Her soft smile calmed the nerves jolting like lightning through his body and subdued the turbulent ocean in his stomach.

Only a little.

Price squeezed her hands and focused, trying with great difficulty to ignore the scrutinizing gaze of the men and the haughty smirk of his brother. He closed his eyes and exhaled. "If we survive the capture of the schooner, if we survive escaping the *Peibo del ler San Francisco*'s volley, if we survive the crew's agitation over changing the articles—"

"That's a lot of 'ifs' there," Angela interrupted, smiling.

"Would you," he continued, ignoring the interruption for the sake of his thoughts and bravery. "Would you consider staying here with me?"

Some of the crew uttered teasing noises, but Price blocked them out. He'd deal with them later. All that mattered was Angela's answer.

"I...I..." she stuttered.

Price waited patiently, having experienced the weight of the words himself.

Her soft lips opened to speak again.

"We must go now!" Riley's voice interrupted her.

Damn that man! With a furrow on his brow, Price turned to his quartermaster. "Not now!"

"The warship is shifting position. If we are to succeed, we have no time to lose!"

Gritting his teeth, the captain shouted his orders, "Vanguard, to the longboats. We take our prize now!"

Such terrible timing, but the future was here—whether they saw tomorrow, and whether Angela would remain at his side.

30

Chapter 30

Smooth quiet oar strokes brought them closer to both the English schooner and the *Peibo del ler San Francisco*. Lanterns lit the warship, and Angela kept a fearful eye on the movements on deck. The moon hid behind cloud cover, giving the vanguard the needed head start. Angela sat next to William in the first longboat. Henry sat at the bow across from her.

The butterflies wrestling in her stomach weren't just about the ships or the impending attack. Henry's question had been so loaded her brain misfired attempting to answer. She'd given him mumbles, just like how he'd asked, which was endearingly sweet.

Captain Henry Price asked her to make a massive life-changing decision for him. She hadn't understood what he'd meant by 'crew's agitation over changing the articles' until after she'd thought about it. Not only did he want her to remain in the past, but he wanted her to stay with him *here*. On the *Sea Lion*. Even if he could get the crew to agree to change the articles for her, Angela was certain she didn't want to sail forever.

Or after this wild adventure, sail after next week.

Angela's palm cupped the necklace's bulge in her pocket. There was a strong chance the necklace was a one-way ticket, anyhow. No more movie nights with her friends. No more burgers and fries. No more camping with Emily—on an air mattress, natch. No more driving a forklift and slinging cases of merchandise with Marcos. No more visiting her mother's grave site.

Mostly, she missed Emily.

She would give anything to have that woman back in her life.

Could Angela give up hope of ever seeing her best friend again and forget returning home, in exchange for a man who treated her well, kept her safe, and drove her wild with sexual need she hadn't felt in so long—making her feel decades younger?

Henry made it possible for her to be one of them, among his crew, his friends, *almost* an equal. His brother appreciated her—or at least her bobby pins. Was all this possible?

Captain Henry Price was everything Brandon Spindleton was not. When Angela had boarded the tour ship, she wanted one night with a captain. The problem was—one night wasn't enough anymore.

Henry kept watch ahead, directing the rowers, and Angela noticed he'd avoided eye contact with her since he'd asked. Was he embarrassed for asking? Was he ashamed she couldn't answer him?

As they neared the warship, a flurry of activity on board churned in her stomach, and dread settled in her bones. Sails were shifting while men rotated the anchor's capstan, and the rest were doing who knew what.

The longboat oars sank below the surface and stroked as silently as the soft waves lapping on shore. Dwarfed by the warship, the English schooner moored peacefully behind its stern. It had ten gunports on her starboard side, so Angela assumed ten on the other, and mounted to the rail were six swivel guns. A handful of Spaniard guards stood sentry on her deck. The schooner was larger and more heavily armed than the *Sea Lion*, ignoring the repair work.

Henry held out a hand to stop the rowers. The second longboat eased alongside, and men from both boats grasped each other's rails to steady them.

The captain addressed the men in their boat, "We shall approach on the port side and climb as quietly as possible. Riley," he addressed the head of the second boat, "have your men climb starboard. When as many men as possible are ready, we'll slip over the rail together, taking her over on swift feet. Our silence is pivotal to our success. If Spain's warship catches a whisper of our activity, she shall train her guns on her own prize, and we shall be finished."

Riley nodded, and Henry gestured for the rowing to resume.

"Are you ready, brother?" Henry asked.

"I'm always ready for a fight, especially for one where we have the upper hand. Strategy is a luxury we shall not squander on this night."

"Are you ready, Angela?" Henry asked, finally meeting her gaze.

Angela's stomach churned like the angry sea from her arrival, and her head swam like when she dove off the *Peibo del ler San Francisco*. Her hands trembled, but the hammer squeezed in her grip stayed steady. Somewhere deep down, an electrifying rush pumped through her veins, preparing her for what was to come. It was adrenaline, and boy, was it welcome. "I'm ready."

Henry leaned close and captured her hands, in full view of the whole vanguard. "Excellent. When this is over, no matter your answer, I'm giving you a kiss."

Heat flourished at her cheeks and chest, and Angela refrained from fanning the front of her tunic. "Promise?" she teased.

William grinned sheepishly beside her. Other men snickered...quietly.

"Certainly, and I never break a promise."

Angela flustered, wanting to dive for him right there, but she refrained.

"Except to me, dear brother," William said.

Henry ignored his brother's jab, so she did too. "Then save some energy for me. You'll need it."

The vanguard cackled. William snorted and shoved Henry on the shoulder. Henry grinned, ignoring their reactions. He rubbed her hands with his thumbs and released her.

Angela darted William a look, and the other brother tilted his head away and scratched at the scruff covering his lower face as if he were innocent. The rowers also tilted their faces aside playfully as if pretending to have not heard the conversation either—almost like they were...friends.

Within reach of the schooner's bow, Henry held up his hand to stop the rowers once again. He reached for a handhold on the schooner's hull and gently eased them alongside.

William slipped the longboat's anchor below the surface and allowed the line to slide in his palm. When the lined stopped, he twisted it around a cleat on the rim of the longboat. The men climbed out, and Angela swallowed back bile as she gripped the ship's hull, waiting.

The second longboat, having delivered the pirates to the starboard side of the ship, reappeared at the stern and signaled them to charge. The longboat returned to position, so the last man could join.

Silently, they tipped themselves over the rail, one after the other, filling the deck from both sides. Clouds shifted, allowing the moon to shine rays on the deck. Blades of metal glinted in the blue light. Men dropped from stab wounds before they drew their own swords. Bodies thumped to the floor, and limp hands released their metal, clattering to the hardwood.

Whispers and grunts alerted other soldiers to the muted attack, and men rushed from below deck, swords drawn. The pirates took on the soldiers with metal clashing in the night. Angela's job was to protect the longboat on her side from soldiers attempting to escape or attempting to remove their chance of escape. She gripped the hammer like her life depended on it, and the shifting and swinging skirmishes around her kept her alert and skittish.

While scanning the deck for anyone attempting to rush her way, she found her attention drifting to Henry. His blade slashed through the air, clashing against his opponent. The urge to rush over and assist threatened to overpower her. Before she realized, Angela left her post and shouldered the hammer. Ducking and dodging the fights around her, and keeping her eyes alert for incoming threats, Angela approached the man fighting Henry and swung at his side.

The man arched his back in crippling pain and dropped his sword. He hugged his side and toppled over the rail, splashing into the waters below.

Henry's chest heaved with exertion, and he lowered the heavy weight in his hand. His soft eyes melted her. "Thank you, my angel." Henry leaned forward and kissed her on the forehead. A quick peck of appreciation and admiration.

Angela smiled. She'd walked through sword fights for him. She'd stolen treasure for him. She'd freed prisoners for him, and she would walk through fire for him, too. Captain Henry Price was the man for her. The answer was yes. Angela would stay here with him.

"Yes!" she blurted with a beaming grin.

"Yes, wha—?" Henry abruptly cut off, eyes widening.

Angela spun to see what caught his attention, and a wounded soldier's pistol aimed straight at them. Without another thought, Angela found herself pulled as the gunshot ripped through the air.

Angela fell and rolled with Henry, who tucked her against his side. His quick hands drew the weapon at his hip, and he aimed and fired at the soldier. The man's hand dropped the gun and hung limp.

Henry said, turning to her. "Are you injured? Have you been struck?"

Angela patted herself just to be sure. "I'm fine. He missed."

"Most excellent." Henry's neck craned around the deck, and he dropped his spent pistol. He fisted another and fired at a man engaged with William.

William swiped his forehead with his sleeve and panted from exertion. The men searched for more opponents, but no more came.

Henry climbed to his feet and held out his hand to help her up. Angela accepted, and as he lifted her, he said, "I'm going to feel that on the morrow."

"No kidding."

"You three," Henry ordered, "check for more below deck. Report back immediately."

Three of the prisoners who'd joined nodded and rushed below deck.

William stepped over bodies, checking them for signs of life. "Your plan worked. Didn't think it would, but I must hand it to you brother, job well done."

"They would've heard the gunshots. The cover of nightfall is our only protection, but since we're very close and they know where they left this ship, we need to weigh anchor at once."

At that, the three of them checked on *Peibo del ler San Francisco*'s position. The warship, with weak winds, slowly approached their old ship. When day broke, they would be capable of aiming and firing. Their current position allowed them to volley both the schooner and the *Sea Lion*.

"And there's much to be done before we're safely underway. I want four men, each boat. Return to shore and collect our supplies and the treasure. The rest of you, put on the soldiers' coats, cravats, and cocked hats and dispose of the bodies. We need to look like them."

Clever. Gross, but clever. The men immediately set to work.

"Angela," Henry said, interrupting her hunt for the cleanest coat. "You owe me a kiss."

"You already stole one," she said teasing.

"That doesn't count." His lips fell upon hers with a deep hungry need, working at her lips like they were the only two people in the world. All the bloodshed and danger around her vanished. For that sweet-but-too-short moment, the only thing in her life was him, and all she wanted was him. All the pain of her past simply became petty. Why had she allowed the humiliation of a bunch of strangers to hurt so much? They wanted her to be someone she wasn't—a square peg in a round hole.

But here, with Henry Price, he was her square hole. An odd thought, but with his soft and sensual lips taking her over, his hands on her ass pulling her toward his stiffening cock, her brain hardly strung linear thoughts. But she believed with every fiber in her body, Captain Henry Price would never abandon her.

Angela pulled back and grinned. "I'm your *numero uno*."

Henry opened his mouth to answer, but something thumped against the hull of the schooner, and that got his attention. Angela pulled away from Henry's sweet embrace. "What was that?"

IT DIDN'T SOUND LIKE cannon fire to her, but Angela wasn't completely sure what it sounded like. Her only experience had been watching movies.

Henry pressed his lips thin and gazed across the deck. "The longboat returning too hastily. The imbecile ruined a perfectly good moment."

"No." Angela smiled, moving back into Henry's arms. "He just gave me a chance to tell you something."

Henry waited patiently, gazing into her eyes as if trying to read the answers on her retinas.

Unlike the nerves warning her away from her doomed wedding, Angela was calm—excited, but calm—and she lifted her arms and wrapped them around his neck. "I tried to tell you earlier—"

"What is it?" He stared at her like she was the only person in the world. Men climbed aboard with arms full of supplies, ignoring them.

Angela's heart swelled, and she swallowed back the emotion clogging her throat. "Yes. I tried to tell you my answer is yes. I will stay with you, Henry."

Her captain grinned for a joyous few seconds before planting another, deeper kiss on her lips. Any deeper and they were going to need a private room. He leaned his body into hers, but a few whistles broke them apart. Nose to nose, his gentle eyes met hers. He smiled and gave her yet another quick peck on the lips. "You have made me the happiest man on this ship."

Angela made a point to glance at the remaining bodies around them. She chuckled. "That doesn't mean much right now."

Henry looked at the bodies too. "I mean to say, you have made me the happiest living man on this ship."

Heckles from the moving crew broke them apart. Angela stood up straight and smoothed her clothing. The trio returned from below deck. "Sir, uh, captain sir," the first one said, trying hard to cover his grin. "The ship is all clear of enemy soldiers, sir."

"Excellent work. Assist with the provisions," Henry said.

Another longboat bumped the hull again, and the trio assisted hoisting the barrels up over the rail. Giles the cook climbed up with great effort, and Captain Price rushed over to give him a hand. Giles settled his feet sturdy on deck, face red with the effort. "This load is the last of our supplies. We can get underway when the boats are secured on board."

"Excellent news, Giles. Take inventory of the provisions below deck. We should have enough to reach our next destination."

"Aye, sir."

"McKee!" Henry called for his master gunner, who immediately approached, still stuffing his arms in a too-tight Spanish coat. "Collect Gunner and inspect the guns and our stock of shot. I want numbers."

The master gunner nodded and walked away, still struggling into a coat.

"Karl." Henry tapped the passing boatswain on the shoulder. "Set sail at once. With the *Peibo del ler San Francisco* encroaching upon the *Sea Lion*, we must get underway. I want the hard in the distance when she opens fire at dawn."

Karl nodded and shouted for hands to assist. Men climbed the ratlines and unfurled the sails from the stays while others raised the anchor.

"What about me?" Angela asked, feeling useless.

"I want you to stay by my side," the captain said with a proud smile. "I never want you out of my sight again."

Angela smiled, equally proud to stand at his side.

"But," he added, leading her toward the stern of the ship, "I remember you claiming if you'd have commanded the ship's helm, the *Sea Lion* wouldn't have wrecked against the outcrop. Care to prove your word?"

A rush of excitement flooded her limbs, and her lips spread wide in a beaming grin. "Oh, yes, I want to sail! Can I?" The idea of driving this behemoth ship made her turn to jelly with ridiculous excitement.

Henry stopped near a serious man, gripping the wheel. "Angela, this is our esteemed Hodgens. He will grant your wish. Hodgens, allow our special guest to take her to sea."

Hodgens pressed his lips thin but nodded once.

Henry said to her, "If you need me, I'll be nearby. Enjoy yourself."

Angela's smile stung her face, but she couldn't relax. Move over forklift. Holding a hundred tons of power in her hands was a thrill like nothing else. Angela bounced on her heels, ready to fly across the seas.

"Be mindful of what you're doing here, lady. It's not child's play. Now, keep your eye on the wind. Spain shall be after us the instant they notice their prize missing, so if those sails start flapping, we start slowing. Understood?"

Angela nodded.

"The vane will help you capture the wind. Adjust your trajectory as I order, and when you need a break, let me know before letting go."

Angela frowned. Way to put a damper on the fun. "I got it. What do I do?"

"When the sails fill, keep the bowsprit aimed where we want to go." Hodgens pointed to the horizon, away from nearby islands.

"Where *are* we going?"

"East to Hispaniola."

Angela steered as directed, squinting straight into the breaking dawn, giving the warship a wide berth. Up ahead, Spain opened the gunports on the starboard side and loaded cannons were pulled into position and aimed. The poor *Sea Lion* had no chance against that ship, and neither did Angela's ears. The thunderous booms of the full broadside echoed off the rocky cliff. One after another after another. Then two came and two more. Wood splintered and splashed. Angela tucked an ear against her shoulder and flinched at the pain, but she wouldn't release the wheel.

Devastating explosions of wood cracked in the air. The mast shattered and toppled. Sails collapsed and draped over the listing deck, and the seawater churned, swallowing the last of their old ship. Cannon smoke filled the area, allowing the English schooner to skirt on by.

Chapter 31

Captain Price found Riley busy in the navigation room, plotting their course out of danger. It was most fortunate for the crew the new three-masted ship was greater in size and strength than the *Sea Lion*, but because of the schooner's size, they'd lost speed and a shallower draft. Once they fully escaped Spain's reach, Riley should be most pleased. When Price closed the door behind him, the quartermaster looked up with a seriousness Price hadn't seen in the younger man. That shall serve him well.

"You sent for me?" Price asked.

Riley set down the quadrant and divider and folded his hands over the map—once Price's but now Riley's, a change that made him wistful. Watching the *Sea Lion*'s destruction had brought tears to his eyes, but he hid them from the others. It was a goodbye in more ways than one, but toward a future rife with a woman he adored.

Riley nodded for him to sit, so Price rested on a chair across from his desk.

"How is your wound?"

"Better every day." Price was grateful Angela had patched him up, and he'd healed without any difficulty. He credited her for saving his life too many times to count.

"Wonderful. You know, if your plan to raid the Spanish treasure failed, I declared I would be their captain, and I had their full support. But you returned one load successfully, and per the articles, we have more than enough to break up the account."

Price had been concerned the crew would disallow his request and maroon him for abandoning the account, but the news sounded favorable. "Not a soul on board contests my request?"

"The crew has accepted, and Hispaniola stands three days hence. But everyone currently aboard, aside from the obvious Angela, decided to continue the account without your leadership. We lost many great men but gained more I hope to see flourish upon these waters." Riley leaned back in his seat. "Only a short time ago I was a child, appreciated by the crew and voted to represent their needs against the captain. I must admit, these tumultuous times have aged me, and you were the best captain I've ever known. I'm going to miss you and certainly your objective"—Riley tilted his head and smiled—"*and* biased decisions in the interest of the crew."

Price blinked away the tears pricking his eyes. He'd never considered goodbye to be so difficult, but he wanted Riley to have the same secret Captain Lemoine had bestowed upon him, just in case. "Noah, there's something I need to tell you. It's about Angela. Do you remember Emily Porter?"

Riley nodded, pulling up chaotic memories. "I remember the captain taking lashes for a woman who'd disguised herself as a man. She was in front of our faces the whole time, and only Fergus knew, may he rest in peace."

"Emily and Angela were friends."

"I'm aware. It's all the other called for."

"They're from the same place."

Riley leaned forward again. "Just spit it out. What is so important about them?"

Price couldn't just spit it out. The man would laugh at him or kick him off the ship prematurely for such a tall tale. "Have you noticed their speech patterns and accent?"

"Yea." Riley frowned. "Never thought much about it."

"They're from the future. Their necklaces, those amethyst stones—they brought the women through time."

Riley stared.

He blinked and continued staring.

Still no response.

"Say something," Price insisted.

"You want me to believe magic necklaces bring women to the past?"

"It's happened twice. I want to warn you as Lemoine did for me. If another woman appears on this ship, understand she's lost, scared, and from a time completely foreign to us. Take care of her. You never know what may transpire."

Riley rubbed his face, clearly not believing him. "I'm the quartermaster. If anyone stows away on this ship—"

"She's not a stowaway!" Price interrupted. "I'm trying to explain to you she's not a stowaway. She simply...appears."

Riley sighed. "If the woman *appears*, I'll make sure the captain is agreeable to her presence and stop the crew from tearing itself to pieces over it."

Price nodded. "Thank you. Have you heard from Vallo at all?"

"No. He must've been lost on Cuba."

As long as Vallo stayed clear of Price's crew, he'd rest peacefully at night. "The man is a traitorous snake. I'm sure Cantu, Buckley, and Hodgens—well, maybe not Hodgens—have told you Vallo was an informant for Spain. Don't trust him."

"In that case, may the enemy be swift and just."

"Agreed," Price said. "There's one last favor I must ask of you."

"Name it," Riley said, "and it shall be done."

"Perform the naming ceremony to appease Poseidon. Have this schooner named Angelfish, after my dearest Angela."

Riley nodded, and a gentle smile lifted his lips. "You have my word, and it shall be my honor. You were a good captain, and we'll miss you. Or...most of us will."

Price stood and discreetly swiped his eyes. "If you need me or Angela, we'll be in my cabin."

Riley stood and stretched out a hand to shake. "Good luck to you both. You're a lucky man."

"I know it." Price shook firmly. Not every day a woman of the future fell into his hands. Certainly not one like her, and he wasn't going to waste a moment of it.

"Also, don't forget to take your share from the barrels left below deck. Not only did we pilfer Spain's recovered treasure and manage to bring it on board, but some poor nation just lost several barrels of gold and silver left on this schooner. Oh, and Price?"

Price stepped back, wishing to further hide his emotion.

"Don't rock the boat." Riley winked.

Price chuckled.

Borrowing the captain's cabin, Henry held the door open for Angela to walk through, but before she crossed, he said, "It's customary for the groom to carry his bride over the threshold."

Angela stopped and turned to him, brows knitting in confusion. Certainly Angela misheard. She couldn't forget such a momentous moment.

Henry continued, "But as this isn't our marital home, and I have not yet asked for your hand, I'm allowing you to walk on your own vocation."

Angela stared, breathless. He'd just told her he intended to ask her to marry him. Advance notice, so this time, she could answer him more swiftly. She supposed no one wanted to wait hours for the answer to a proposal.

Henry led her by the hand into the quarters and closed the door. With sunlight glittering through the bank of windows at the stern, he collected her hands in his. Bright ocean blue eyes met her gaze, and all the best things projected from his beautiful face. Henry was excited but serious and full of adoration, and she caught a hint of nervousness. Angela's breath caught, and her knees were weak. He was doing it now, she knew it.

"Before I met you, I was a jaded man on a mission surely to end in my demise. So long as my vengeance had been finished, I cared not what happened to me. With my brother presumed dead, I had no reason to live." Angela squeezed his hands in sympathy for his suffering.

He rubbed her knuckles in return. "But you, my angel, you gave me a purpose, and now I fear losing you more than anything else. Angela, my lady, I love you, and I don't want to spend one more day on this earth without you. Will you do me the honor of becoming my *numero uno* forever?"

Tears flooded her eyelids, and she furiously blinked them away. Henry was a real man, bleeding his heart out for her with words that turned her to mush and reminded her that kindness and true love still existed. When she'd donned the magic necklace, her wish had been to never see another cell phone again, but deep down she wished to meet someone special. She had.

"Are you asking what I think you're asking?"

"Marry me," he said simply.

"Captain Henry Price," she began slowly, formally, trying to keep her emotions in check to finish her statement. "You are the best person I've ever met. You're kind, considerate, and more handsome than I ever hoped for, but—" she paused when Henry's wide smile of anticipation threatened to interrupt "—you're also a great leader and a strong fighter, and I feel safe with you. I love you more than I thought possible. I have your answer, and you were right to assume I needed time to decide."

Henry's smile waned a little, but he didn't interrupt.

"I never wanted to stay on a ship. The crew life isn't for me, but handling the helm has its perks, and for you, my Henry, my answer is yes. I'll stay with you forever, and I'm thrilled to marry you." Tears wavered her vision. She blinked them back to see his reaction. His features melted with happiness, and his arms opened to embrace her. "Absolutely, yes," Angela repeated, smiling, and swiped her tears.

Henry scooped her up into a tight embrace. The world could fall apart around them, but as long as she had her captain by her side, they could conquer anything—even a sinking ship, an angry crew, and a warship full of vengeful enemy soldiers. Henry shifted his hands to her throat and jawline. He took her lips with the gusto of a man ready to possess her in new ways. The articles forbade such acts on board, for the equality of the crew, so Angela stopped him when he motioned her toward the bed.

"We're so close to disembarking. I'd hate to cause a crisis with the crew now," Angela said. The wait had been its own kind of torture, but the building anticipation meant when the main event happened, it was going to be glorious. Angela felt something pressing against her, and ignoring the part that was clearly Henry's excitement, she dug in her pocket.

Henry groaned at her continued rejection. "You're right. Riley is just getting his feet wet; he doesn't need the crew rallying. Rules are rules."

Angela backed up with a frown and stuck her hand in her pocket.

"What is it?" Henry asked, concern taking over.

Angela palmed the amethyst on a copper chain.

"Your way home?" Henry asked.

"Not anymore." Angela moved to the captain's private head, lifted the lid, and with a deep breath, she dropped the necklace straight into the ocean. She returned to the captain's embrace. His strong arms circled her. "That never truly was home."

32

Chapter 32

THE HORSES' HOOVES CLOPPED against the dirt path leading away from the dock, pulling her and Henry in a tight covered carriage. Suspension was definitely not a thing yet. In the captain's quarters of the schooner, a chest had held various gowns, and Henry insisted she wear one. Despite the fluffy layers acting as cushion, her butt was getting sore. She adored the dress, even more so after wearing ill-fitting, sodden, salty, scratchy men's clothing. Even her sweat work polo wasn't as bad.

Her top was a ruffled ivory blouse, and the bottom was layers of gold. The boned corset had embroidered swirls in the gold, and she felt like a regal princess. Henry wore a black tunic with a similar patterned coat and black breeches, a gentleman on the outside like she knew he was on the inside.

At this distance up a hill, Angela could make out men refitting the new schooner, preparing to set sail once again. She was going to miss it. Well, parts of it, like Buckley and Cantu, and the beautiful sunrises and sunsets.

Not so much the jungle bugs, the hard night's sleep, Vallo and his tricks, and the Spanish threat. Whatever happened to Vallo? Ultimately, it didn't matter, she supposed.

When Henry had said Riley was just getting his feet wet, he'd meant Riley was taking temporary command until a new captain could be elected. Henry didn't want to remain on the sea, either. She would've done it for him, honestly, but she was glad they wanted the same thing.

Henry held her hand during the rocky ride, and dust kicked up behind them. This was their first moment of privacy, without the risk of death, since they'd met. Angela couldn't help her eyes from drifting to his peeking chest hair.

"Is something the matter, my lady?" Henry asked with a saucy tone.

Heat rushed to her cheeks and pooled lower, far lower, where she'd been aching for attention. "Can we take a detour? Somewhere private."

Clothing shifted in Price's lap. "Are you needing something at this moment?"

"Oh, yes. Very much."

"I think we have time for something." Henry held his hand out for her, and she took it without a second thought. He pulled her into his lap, and a firm length greeted her, bouncing with the uneven road under the carriage. Henry groaned.

Angela gasped. The throbbing between her legs, matching her increasing heartbeat, made her want to tear off every last shred of destroyed clothing on his body.

As her lips fell upon his, Angela slipped her hands up his tunic. She blindly explored the ridges of his chest, the rings dangling from his nipples, the softness of his skin, but she avoided his bandaged wounds. Henry was perfect, and now it was her turn to groan. "Are you sure we have enough time? I'm going to need a week."

Henry laughed and his thick hands gripped her butt and pressed her closer. His thick cock eagerly awaited her. "Let us enjoy one quick round. And I promise you many more to come."

She'd take what she could get. Angela was feeling downright feral by now. She lifted her layers of dress and Henry untied his breeches and loosened them enough. She dug at the ties on his underwear, releasing his length. Angela spit in her palm and lubed him up, which surprised him. But his reaction may have been for her touch, rather than her action. She wasn't going to stop and analyze proper lady bedroom etiquette in the back of a bumpy carriage ride.

Gripping his hard cock, Angela lowered herself onto him, and Henry moaned with pleasure, and she cried out.

At once she started to grind against him, and Henry captured her lips. He wouldn't let go, and she had no intention of leaving this carriage until she exploded from the built tension she'd carried since she first laid eyes on him. He was her anchor. She was his *number uno*.

Forever.

Angela smoothed the rat's nest of hair on her head and attempted to smooth her dress, which was nearly impossible in the carriage. Her face was flushed red from the exertion, and she couldn't stop smiling. Henry's own face was peaceful and relaxed while he tucked his tunic into his breeches. When this surprise was over, she needed at least two more rounds to be satisfied.

A vast seaside plantation appeared over the hill. The horses followed the long driveway and stopped with the carriage aligned with the fancy front door. Henry had promised her a surprise, but since he wanted to settle in the colonies on the mainland, she wasn't sure what this stately manor was about, and he refused to tell her.

The driver circled around and opened their door, offering a hand to Angela. His delicate treatment was so strange to her, but out of politeness, she accepted the assistance.

Henry climbed out behind them and, recollecting her hand and folding it around his arm, he led her up the short stairs and knocked. While waiting for the door to be answered, he asked, "Do you have a...phone...on you?"

Absently, Angela said, "Yeah, but the saltwater fried it. Plus, the battery's dead. I hate phones, anyway..." She trailed off and stared at him. "You know what a phone is?"

Henry only smiled with amusement, and the front door opened. A woman in a drab-colored dress folded her hands together and said, "Master Lemoine and Mistress Porter shall see you now. Right this way." She stepped back and waited for them to entered.

Angela's features twisted at the titles—master and mistress. She visualized many bedroom images. Her mind was already heavily focused on Henry, she didn't need more creative thoughts plaguing her while she needed to be a lady. She gripped Henry's forearm tighter.

Henry led them into a vast entryway with vases, flowers, and a delicate chandelier. Impressive.

The woman, Angela guessed a housekeeper, stopped and gestured toward a room.

Henry brought her over the threshold, where two people sat in antique upholstered chairs with intricate carvings. Their clothing was extravagant, considering the heat of the tropics, and Angela's excessive, but appreciated, dress fit right in. She uselessly smoothed her ratty hair, and when the lady of the house set down a teacup and rose to face her, Angela's hand stilled. She blinked several times and tilted her head, squinting at the familiar face in an unfamiliar world.

After all that time at sea, now she was hallucinating. "Em?"

The woman beamed with recognition and rushed toward her with fistfuls of cumbersome dress. Her arms opened wide, and Emily crashed against Angela.

"It's really you?" Angela asked, tears flooding her eyes. "You're really here?"

"Ange! I missed you so much. We have so much to talk about! I thought I lost you."

Angela sobbed and turned to Henry. His eyes were pink with his own emotion, and he smiled gently.

On the beach after the wreck, when Angela was worried for her mental health, Henry had told her he knew how different this was for her. Not difficult. *Different.* He knew where she was from. He knew all along, and that was the real reason he protected her...and brought her the greatest gift.

"You knew?" she asked him. "After all this time, you knew Emily was here? Why didn't you tell me?"

Henry said, "Is there a time you could've gotten here on your own?"

He had a point. Angela would've been distraught trying to find her way here, and she probably wouldn't have made it, not without Henry. She smiled at him in thanks.

Henry returned her smile, and he approached the man of the house, who also wore fancy threads. They shook hands and embraced, patting each other on the back, like long-lost friends.

Angela turned back to her friend. "I searched for you, but no one heard of you, except Henry. For a while, I thought I was going crazy."

"The necklaces were real magic. I still can't believe it myself. Still have yours?"

"Dropped it down the toilet. You?"

"Tossed it off the coast in Nassau."

Angela laughed and admired her friend's dress. "You hate dresses. What are you wearing?"

Emily chuckled. "It takes some getting used to. I tripped on these layers so many times. Good thing I tossed that necklace, or I would've been tempted to use it again to buy some jeans."

Angela laughed. "Good thing Robin never showed up. That girl doesn't do well without control."

"Could you picture her in this time? She'd go crazy."

Emily shook her head. "Come on, let me introduce you."

Angela took her friend's arm, and they crossed the room, approaching the men.

Henry and his friend pulled apart from their hug.

"Angela, this is my husband, Eric Lemoine. Eric, my best friend, Angela Foxe."

Lemoine took her hand, and on a bow, he kissed her knuckles. "The pleasure is all mine. I've heard of the missing Angela for so long, it's a relief to see you are well. And my friend, my old quartermaster, you've left the sea?"

Henry captured Angela's hand back from his friend. "I caught myself the best treasure a man could ask for. I have no use for the black any longer. I must tell you of our exploits in Cuba. Spain recovered barrels of gold from the treasure galleon's wreck. We found where they'd hid it, and we collected it first."

"Congratulations. I suspect you'll be wanting for nothing now," Lemoine said.

"No, and I have Angela here to thank for saving my brother's life."

Emily stared at her.

Lemoine's brows lifted in surprise. "You found William *alive*?"

Angela said, "Spain locked him in the hold of the *Peibo del ler San Francisco*, awaiting delivery for trial, but he escaped. Never underestimate the value of bobby pins."

Emily laughed. "Come. You must sit and share tea. It's not as good as the modern stuff, but you'll get used to it. Tell us all about what happened to you after you put on the necklace."

Angela took Henry's hand and together they sat and regaled their tales at sea. Emily told her tale as well, and Angela's life couldn't have been more perfect.

33

Chapter 33

THE CREW, OLD AND new, circled around Riley as he finished speaking the oath to Poseidon to remove all references of the schooner's given name from the Ledger of the Deep. He and Cantu poured a serving of champagne directly into His Majesty's sea. The men cheered, and Riley spoke the prayers to appease the gods of the four winds in the name of the *Angelfish*.

More champagne was dumped overboard, and upon the ceremony's completion, the crew eagerly guzzled down the remaining sparkling drink.

Buckley and his new carpenter's mate collected an armful of painting supplies to change the name emblazoned on the hull.

"Buckley, Watts, wait for a few moments more," Riley said, and addressed the officers. "We have Price, the armorer, returning to us. Hodgens shall continue to steer us. McKee shall lead the gun crew. Giles, our esteemed cook, we couldn't do this without you. Karl, you allow us to move along the sea. But we must vote for the captain and quartermaster to lead us on the new account."

"You're not staying with us?" Buckley asked.

"Much has transpired as of late, and I believe it is only fair that all voices are heard and agreed before we set sail on a new account. Now, in the matter of quartermaster, who are the nominees?"

McKee stepped forward. "I've been told you're going to vote for me, but I must assure all you fine men, I don't want it. Guns are my specialty and where I find I'm at my best. I vote for Karl Dillon."

Men cheered, and Boatswain Karl stepped forward with a placating gesture. "And I assure you all dirty rats, the quartermaster is not for me either. I must respectfully decline."

The men booed.

John Randall, a rescued prisoner, stepped forward next. "I was quartermaster under four captains on the Queen's Defiance over the course of several years, and although my crews trusted me fully, I understand that none of you know me. I offer myself as the nominee, because that is my best function."

The crew mumbled among themselves.

Riley thought it only a matter of formality that he'd step forward. Quartermaster was the position he'd been most comfortable with, but during an emergent situation, he felt empowered to handle the captaincy, and he'd allowed his dreams take hold. But that situation was no longer. "I nominate myself, in case you sea dogs have forgotten my many accomplishments for this crew."

The men laughed.

Riley added, "If no one else cares to step forward, we shall begin with the vote. All those in favor of Randall, say aye."

Many hands and ayes accompanied nods, which surprised Riley.

"And in favor of myself?"

No ayes. Dead silence. The wind was pulled from his chest, like an unexpected meaty fist to the gut. Riley's eyes settled on Cantu, whose enormous arms folded over his chest. Not even the gentle giant wanted Riley to retain his position.

The crew thought less of him than the newest recruit or the master gunner. How could that be? Steeling himself against the rejection, Riley exhaled quietly and said, "Then Randall is our new quartermaster. Let us pray your vast experience helps us greatly."

The men clapped and cheered the result while a crushing pain settled on Riley's shoulders. After all these years, from a young man to what he'd thought was leadership material, they'd shunned him. When the vote for captain was complete, he wasn't going to stay with the crew.

Riley still had his dignity. "Now for your captain. Nominees step forward."

The crew turned their heads back and forth like guilty children who didn't want to tattle on each other. Not a soul stepped forward. Not a soul spoke up.

"Anyone at all care to lead this crew?"

Cantu stepped forward, and Riley sighed in relief. He trusted the man, who'd proven time and again to have the crew's loyalty. "We only want *you* to lead us, Riley. We already decided unanimously. No need for the formal vote."

Riley cleared his throat and tried several times to swallow the lump forming. "You're certain? All of you...want me?"

"You showed great courage and strength facing Captain Price while on enemy territory. You handled a precarious position with a straight head and narrow focus, and we respected your actions. Despite your close relationship with the captain, you made decisions in everyone's best interests rather than trying to salvage your friendship. The mark of a great leader is in you. We trust you to lead us now into further victory."

"My age doesn't bother you?" Riley was six and twenty years of age, younger than most on the ship.

"Age is nothing but a number. It's the head on your shoulders that counts," Cantu said.

Captain Noah Riley? A voted captain, not one taken by force. *Captain...* The word repeated in his head, having never processed the title included before. These men wanted him to lead them to riches. He'd do whatever it took to show these men a grand time and riches beyond belief. For granting him his dignity and putting their full trust in him, he would reward them.

"Well, what are you waiting for?" Riley asked, slipping into his new role seamlessly. "Paint *Angelfish* on the hull at once. Swab the deck, and weigh anchor. We set sail at dawn, on the trail of riches."

Now that daydream could come true.

34

Epilogue

VALLO RUBBED HIS EYES and climbed up to the main deck of the *Peibo del ler San Francisco*. He'd remained hidden while Spain had taken great losses last night, so what was one more? After Vallo had stashed his treasure on the English schooner, he sought safety aboard the warship until the perfect moment to commandeer the smaller vessel for his own use.

That time had come.

The sun blinded him. Holding his hand to shield his view, the seas were calm, both a blessing and a curse. The ship wasn't moving as quickly as he liked, but in light winds, the schooner would have an advantage. Vallo crossed amidships, and on the port side, the endless seas surrounded them.

Vallo frowned.

At the stern, figuring the smaller ship to stay in its place, Vallo still failed to find it. His heart thundered in his chest. All his treasure was on that ship. He rushed around the soldiers and knocked on the captain's door. Upon his approval to enter, Vallo rushed inside and closed the door.

Capitán Delgado sipped from a flute of champagne, and Vallo's throat was suddenly dry.

"What is the matter, Vallo?" the captain asked in Spanish.

"Where is the schooner?"

The captain leaned forward, face darkening with anger. "You tell me."

"I...I..." Vallo trailed off. He wouldn't tell the man what he'd planned. "What do you mean?"

"The prisoners from this ship broke free and stole my prize. Do you know anything about that?"

"Me? No. They were enemies. I gave them nothing. Are we heading in pursuit?"

"This warship was built for defense and destruction. There is no propulsion system known to man capable of bringing this ship within broadside distance of the schooner. Those pirates had stolen the schooner we captured and stolen Spain's treasure. By explaining their actions, I may find some level mercy, but the repercussions from the Crown to myself are expected to be of grave consequence."

Vallo fished out the meaning. "You're not pursuing the schooner or Price's crew?"

"I cannot."

Vallo gritted his teeth and left the cabin. He stalked over to the rail and searched the horizon for the sails of his enemies. Unlike Delgado, Vallo wouldn't allow the pirates to get the best of him. Spain had no idea Vallo had taken more of their treasure than he'd been allowed, and Spain wasn't going to help him retrieve it.

Vallo would never sleep until he had his treasure back, and he intended to slay every man on board that schooner to do it. Although...if he considered his plans more carefully, he needed a small crew just to sail her. So the ones most deserving of their lives and pledging the hardest shall be spared, only until he reached land and found a new crew of his own.

Price, Riley, and the rest of the *Sea Lion* crew and all the escaped prisoners, especially that woman, were all on his list to dispatch. First, they were going to experience the worst torture known to pirates at Vallo's own hand, and he would not sleep until his quest was complete.

They all needed to pay.

Dear Reader,

DIVE INTO ROBIN HALL and Captain Riley's story in **Pirate's Plunder (Pirates in Time Book 3)**!

As an indie author, I'm thrilled you decided to share your time with me, exploring the crazy worlds residing in my head and keeping me up at night. Your reviews are very important to me, so if you enjoyed this book, please consider leaving some stars for Angela Foxe and Captain Price's story, **Pirate's Treasure (Pirates in Time Book 2)**.

If you found any typos or errors, I blame my cat. Rat her out at: support@stephanieflynn.com.

Thank you for your support!

Also By Stephanie Flynn

Find my catalog at StephanieFlynn.com
Immortal Protector series
0.5 Vampire's Distraction
1 Vampire's Deception
2 Vampire's Secret
3 Vampire's Promise
3.5 Elf Bound
4 Vampire's Demand

Immortal Protector Side Tales
Deer Holiday
Love Claws
Depths of the Heart

Matchmaker in Time series
0.5 Minutes to Live

1 Seconds to Act
2 Hours to Arrive
3 Days to Hide
4 Years to Savor

Pirates in Time series
1 Pirate's Prize
2 Pirate's Treasure
3 Pirate's Plunder

Time Travel Romance Shorts
Fateful Time
One Crazy Time

If you like your urban fantasy without the romance, too, check out Stephanie Flynn's other name, Marie Flynn!

About Stephanie Flynn

Stephanie Flynn writes action-packed paranormal romance filled with adventure, suspense, and danger. She lives in Michigan, USA, with her husband and kids, and she spends her writing time surrounded by a herd of normal cats who bat everything off her desk, including her coffee. Check out her website for more books: StephanieFlynn.com